S0-BXQ-240

POCKET
PEGASUS

Also by Susan Stafford-Pooley:

POCKET PEGASUS:
Flash and the Turtle Creek Triad

POCKET PEGASUS

Flash
and the
Wings of
Courage

SUSAN STAFFORD-POOLEY

WINGED HORSE BOOKS

WH BOOKS

All rights reserved. No part of this publication may be reproduced, stored in a retrieval system or transmitted, in any form or by any means, without the prior written consent of the publisher.

This novel is a work of fiction. Any resemblance to actual persons or locales is entirely coincidental.

Library and Archives Canada Cataloguing in Publication

Stafford-Pooley, Susan, 1954-
    Pocket Pegasus : Flash and the wings of courage / Susan Stafford-Pooley.

ISBN 978-0-9877608-0-7

    I. Title.

PS8637.T325P63 2011   jC813'.6   C2011-905953-3

© 2011 Susan Stafford-Pooley

WINGED HORSE BOOKS
Amherstburg, Ontario, Canada
www.pocketpegasus.com

Cover illustration by Jean Abernethy
www.JeanAbernethy.com

Printed in Canada.

ACKNOWLEDGEMENTS

Special thanks to Darcy Thachuk, Foster Parent Recruiter at the Windsor-Essex Children's Aid Society, for her honest and informative insights into the important work these agencies perform to protect children and build strong families.

This book is dedicated to all the kids who must find
their own wings of courage,
whatever form or path that takes.

Chapter 1

"Flash!"

Laura Connor squinted against the late summer sun as she looked upwards at the roof of her house. A small, silver figure — a tiny horse with wings — was skittering over the peak of the roof and heading down the other side.

"Get down here! Mom and Dad are going to be home soon. *Geez!*"

Life had been anything but dull since the evening two months earlier when Flash had unexpectedly and explosively come into Laura's life. She thought back to the ear-splitting crack of thunder which had jarred her from sleep as lightning had struck the very roof she was now scanning. The powerful surge of electricity had passed through her special porcelain Pegasus statuette sitting in the windowsill of her bedroom, igniting his soul and reversing an ancient spell.

Now, the result of this incredible twist of fate was ignoring Laura's pleas to get back to his hiding place in her closet.

"I'm having fun. There are squirrels up here." Flash's petulant voice floated down to the lawn. "Once you go back to school I won't be able to have any fun ever again."

Laura snorted. "Of course you will. Now come down before the neighbours see you."

The sight of an eight-inch tall equine chatterbox with wings would certainly cause a stir among the residents of the small Ontario town of Turtle Creek where Laura lived with her parents. Only two other people knew of Flash's existence. One of them was Krissy Martineau, Laura's best friend. Laura could never have kept such an incredible secret from the one person with whom she shared everything cool.

Flash was waiting on the front porch, impatiently hovering like a hummingbird in front of the door. The moment Laura swung it open, he careered through the hallway and up the stairs. Maxine, Laura's plump old tabby cat, thundered after her feathered friend.

Laura exhaled loudly with relief. Summer was drawing to a close and school was starting in just a few days. She had no idea what to do with Flash while she was in class. He was easily bored and was always getting into trouble when left on his own. Her parents, as yet, did not know about their tiny tenant. Laura planned to tell them—some day.

As if keeping such a big secret from her parents wasn't causing enough stress for the thirteen-year-old, Laura was also about to tackle Grade 8 at Turtle Creek District School. She had heard the curriculum was much harder and the teachers were stricter. Plus, she was quite small for her age and was worried how she would fare playing sports with the other girls who all seemed to tower over her. She had even been the victim of some nasty bullying in seventh grade. In short, she felt like a very small fish being dumped into a great big sea.

At least Krissy would be there to listen to her woes. And thankfully, because Turtle Creek District was a "hybrid" school combining grades 7 through 12, Todd Williams— the only other person on the planet who knew about Flash—would be there, too. A grade ahead of Laura and Krissy, Todd was a troubled fourteen-year-old boy who called himself Blade. His failed attempt to abduct Flash weeks earlier had left the magical little equine ruffled but unhurt. After an uneasy truce, Todd and the girls had become fast friends, sealing their vow of secrecy with three bloody thumbprints on a written pact which formed the Turtle Creek Triad.

Laura felt better knowing that Todd would watch her back. He had the reputation of being a loner, "that weird goth kid," but she knew that his dark clothing, gloomy music and black eye makeup was just a way to distance himself from other people. With help from Krissy, Laura, and her family, he had emerged from his shell and had begun to shed his cloak of darkness and anger.

Laura heard a sound on the porch behind her. It was Krissy, out of breath.

"Alba's having her foal! Mrs. Leeds has been trying to get hold of you. Where have you been, anyway?" She inhaled a big, whooping breath. "I ran all the way over. You should keep your cell phone on, for Pete's sake."

Mrs. Leeds owned Banbury Cross Stables, a local farm where Laura had worked all summer. Alba d'Oro, one of her broodmares, was due to foal the following week. Laura had assumed she would miss the birth because it would likely happen at night, as is often the case with horses, or while she was at school.

"That's too cool!" Laura started to pull the front door shut behind her, then froze. "Only problem is, we have no way to get there."

As if on cue, the Connor's van rolled up in the driveway. Laura's father didn't even have a chance to shut the engine off before Laura was down the steps and yanking the passenger door open.

"Mom! I need to get to the farm right now!" She stopped, seeing the shocked look on her mother's face. "Please," she added more politely. "Alba's foaling. Could you take us?"

"Absolutely!" Her mother slid smoothly over to the driver's seat, swinging her hips to hasten her husband's departing backside. "Git! Us girls are on a mission."

Krissy and Laura scrambled into the van and the three midwives roared off into the countryside.

~ ~ ~

Banbury Cross Stables consisted of a lovely old stone house and a tidy array of barns and outbuildings. The main stable was eerily quiet as the threesome tiptoed hurriedly down the aisle toward the roomy foaling stall.

"I've never seen a horse have a baby before," Krissy whispered.

"Me neither," replied Laura and her mother as one.

They joined Mrs. Leeds outside the stall, watching in hushed awe as Alba paced fretfully in circles, stopping occasionally to look at her flanks with her ears pinned.

The mare was sweating and seemed very distressed.

"I hope motherhood improves her disposition," Mrs. Leeds joked under her breath. Alba swung around and gave her a nasty glare, as if she had heard the comment. The girls giggled, then hastily shushed each other.

Within minutes, Alba had settled into the deep, clean straw bedding and was starting to strain.

"Where's the vet?" Laura's mother asked. "Shouldn't he be here?"

Mrs. Leeds replied without taking her eyes off the labouring mare. "I've notified Dr. Anwar. He can be here in a few minutes if there's trouble, but in my experience it's usually best to let nature take its course."

Nature was indeed taking its course without any human help at all. Suddenly, a gauzy sac with a tiny hoof appeared, followed closely by another, with a dainty muzzle resting on top.

"Good, the foal is presented properly." Mrs. Leeds seemed relieved, in spite of her years of experience in the foaling barn. "If the soles of the hooves are facing upwards, in can mean problems, even a breech birth."

"That's backwards," Mrs. Connor volunteered proudly. "I didn't know that could happen to horses, too."

"It does, and sometimes the vet has to try to manually turn the foal around." Laura's mother looked horrified.

"Ow," she said weakly.

Suddenly, there was a load groan, a gush, and the foal slid wetly onto the straw. Mrs. Leeds quickly went into the stall and pulled the amniotic sac away from the foal's nose so that she—or was it a he?—could breathe.

Laura and Krissy were huddled together, lost for words, overwhelmed with the raw intensity of the scene before them.

Alba had raised her head and was gazing with great interest at the new arrival. The soggy foal struggled briefly and the remains of the sac enclosing him fell away, revealing a glossy dark brown coat accented by a small star on his forehead and four white socks.

After a quick and discreet inspection of the foal's nether regions, Mrs. Leeds announced that the baby was indeed a colt, which brought stifled whoops of glee from the girls. Alba suddenly lumbered to her feet and moved protectively between the foal and the stall door.

Mrs. Leeds took Laura's mother aside for a moment. "CeeCee, the mare will likely deliver the placenta in the next few minutes, which is not the prettiest sight. Why don't you take the girls down to the office for a bit? It will give Alba a little quiet time to recover and bond with the foal. I'll tidy things up and they can come back to watch him take his first steps." She thought for a second, then said, "Ask Laura to call the vet and tell him the foal has been born, the mare is fine, and everything is good so far. He will want to come out and inspect them both fairly soon. And," she added, "I could really do with a cup of tea."

The girls were reluctantly herded down the aisle to the cozy stable office for vet-phoning and tea-making duties. They restlessly flipped through old issues of *Horse-Canada* magazine and worked on the crosswords in the *Horsepower* kids' section. CeeCee tiptoed back down the hall to deliver the mug of hot tea to the stable owner, then rejoined the antsy girls in the office.

About twenty minutes later, Mrs. Leeds poked her head in the door and said, "The little guy and his momma are ready for company again."

The foal was in the process of getting a thorough tongue bath by Alba, who had decided this motherhood thing was serious business. Head wobbling and long legs splayed out in front of him, the newborn struggled to get his hind end under him. This accomplished—sort of—he straightened his hocks and pitched drunkenly onto his nose in the deep straw. The concerned gasps from the girls quickly turned to giggles as the next attempt to stand saw him collapse behind and sit on his haunches like a dog.

Slowly, steadily, the little guy managed to get all four legs under him and stood shakily. Alba murmured gently and the foal bobbled over to her side, instinctively looking for his first meal. After a bit of bumping and a few false starts he began nursing, nourishing himself with that important first milk, the colostrum. "That's good," Mrs. Leeds said, satisfied. "Momma's milk will help protect him from diseases. So far, he's done everything right."

As Laura surveyed the scene, she was overcome by the feeling that she was witnessing something so incredibly special, yet so completely natural. She felt privileged to have been given the chance to attend the birth.

She suddenly had a thought. "What are you going to name him?"

Mrs. Leeds smiled. "I've tried to come up with a suitable name, but I'm pretty much open to suggestions. Alba d'Oro means Golden Dawn in Spanish, and his sire is Bikini Bay. Of course, a name honouring both parents would be nice."

You could almost hear the wheels turning in the girls' minds. Mrs. Connor, however, was the first to speak up. "How about Golden Bikini?" she offered.

Laura gave her mother a wilting look. "Oh, Mom, don't you think that's a bit girly-girl for a boy horse?"

CeeCee sighed. "I suppose so. Hey, I'm new at this."

Krissy piped up. "Golden Bay would be better." She corrected herself immediately. "Nope, sounds too much like a coat colour."

Laura giggled. "How does d'Or Key sound?"

This unleashed a torrent of totally silly ideas:

"Golden Thong."

"Skinny Dipper."

"Dawn Juan."

"Tequila Sunrise."

"Tan Lines."

"Some Beach!"

The last one brought gales of laughter, for anyone who was familiar with Alba knew that the broodmare had a rather frosty personality.

"What about Spanish Bay?" Laura was more serious now.

Mrs. Leeds mulled the idea over for a moment. "I like it. I really like it. I'll check with the Jockey Club to see if it's available. He likely won't race, seeing as he was born so late in the year, but I want to register him anyway. Good job, team."

Footsteps in the aisle announced the arrival of the vet. Dr. Anwar, a young graduate who had recently taken over the local practice from a retiring colleague, greeted Mrs. Leeds. The stable owner quickly brought him up to speed on the details of the birth. He nodded, smiled and entered the stall to examine the mare and foal.

Alba immediately nudged the foal over to the far side of the stall, away from the intruder. She pinned her ears and looked positively ferocious. Mrs. Leeds slipped into the stall and snapped a lead rope onto the mare's halter. "Please don't eat the vet," she admonished Alba. She winked at Dr. Anwar. "Good ones are hard to find."

The rest of the exam was relatively uneventful. Satisfied that the mare was fine, Dr. Anwar swabbed the foal's navel stump with iodine solution and pronounced him healthy. As if he understood, the little colt scampered unsteadily across the stall to his mother's side. "Just make sure that he passes the meconium in the next hour or so."

Krissy looked puzzled. "Meconium? What in the world is that?"

Laura gestured to Mrs. Leeds with a sweep of her arm. "Over to you."

"It's the foal's first bowel movement. Very important—it shows that all the systems are working. It's very unusual stuff, sort of brown and tarry—"

"Whoa, TMI," said Krissy, holding up her hands and cringing.

Chapter 2

"You should have seen it! It was the coolest thing *ever*!"

Laura's voice rose with excitement as she recounted the birth to her father over dinner.

"Well, I have seen a birth before," Tom admitted, "but it wasn't a horse, just a horse-crazy girl."

"In case you've forgotten, you fainted," CeeCee reminded him.

Laura's father looked hurt. "Men don't faint," he corrected her. "They pass out. That's what manly men do."

"Whatever." CeeCee laughed. "Call it what you want. You fell in a heap on the floor. That's how I remember it."

CeeCee was dishing out bowls of warm apple crisp when there was a knock at the door. Todd stood on the porch, looking a bit sheepish.

"Oh man, I'm sorry, you're having dinner," he apologized, turning and starting to head back down the steps.

"Don't be ridiculous," Mrs. Connor said, waving him through the door. "Have some dessert with us. There's loads of it." She herded Todd into the kitchen, ignoring his protests, and filled another bowl with fragrant apple slices and cinnamon crumbles.

CeeCee was aware that the tall, shy boy often missed meals and enjoyed spending time with Laura's little family. His own home life consisted of a father who spent too much money on beer and not nearly enough on groceries. Todd often endured verbal and physical abuse, which had become more frequent lately even though he now towered over his father in height. Since his father had been laid off from his job a year earlier, and his mother had walked out and never looked back, the tension between them was becoming worse.

"Todd, are you coming to the concert in the park tonight?" Mrs. Connor asked. "We're playing third in the lineup, about nine o'clock. We're just doing a short set, though, because the headliners are on after us and the whole thing has to be wrapped up by eleven due to the local noise by-laws. Ridiculous," she muttered. "Music's not *noise.*"

"Oh, come with Krissy and me. It'll be fun," Laura said. She rarely got to see her parents perform with their seven-piece band, High Octane, as they were usually playing private events such as weddings and parties. She loved listening to her mother singing the old jazz standards and Motown melodies, although she would never admit to her friends that she actually liked that kind of stuff. Truth be told, she liked every kind of music, even classical, especially when she was alone in her room reading, doing homework, or just watching Flash fly around. If anyone asked, however, she usually gushed about Katy Perry or Taylor Swift or the latest Arcade Fire tunes.

Krissy arrived as Laura's parents were packing up their gear. Laura nodded her head toward the stairs, a gesture Todd and Krissy understood to mean, "We'd better go see what His Highness is up to."

His Highness was pacing impatiently on the dresser, gently fanning his wings to stay cool in the lingering late-summer heat. Laura glanced at her bookcase and noticed that her pretty Breyer Pegasus model horse was laying on its side—again. This seemed to mysteriously happen whenever Flash had been left alone for too long. He became disruptive when he was bored, knocking things over, getting into drawers, turning on the radio, rumbling with the cat. When no one was home he would sneak downstairs and watch *Animal Planet* on the television in the living room. Laura had even caught him trying on old Barbie clothes from the back of her closet. The sight of Flash decked out in a jaunty beret and feather boa had set her off into gales of laughter.

"It's about time," the little winged horse snorted. "I've been waiting for you *forever.*"

"Oh, chill out, bro," Todd said, ruffling Flash's luxuriant mane. "We brought you some apple crumble." He placed the tiny bowl of now-cold dessert in front of their impatient friend. With little sounds of delight, Flash buried his muzzle in the mix of apples, oatmeal and sweet brown sugar. He snarfed and slurped and did not come up for air until the bowl was empty.

"This may be a *huge* mistake," Laura said slowly, "but would you be interested in coming to the fairgrounds with us to watch the concert tonight?"

Flash tilted his head and gave Laura a scornful look. "What do *you* think? Wait, maybe I'd better stay here and keep an eye on the house—*not!*"

Laura pulled her backpack from the closet and Flash slid in obediently. She zipped it partway shut, leaving a gap through which Flash could poke his head whenever the coast was clear.

~ ~ ~

As the trio began the long trek to the fairgrounds, Laura felt Flash wiggling in the backpack over her shoulder and smiled. He had adapted so well to a life that was radically different from the one he had lived with others of his kind thousands of years before. The fact that he had once been a magnificent full-sized winged horse and was now smaller than her cat was perhaps the biggest adjustment he had to bear.

Flash was fascinated by technology, which was new and exciting to him. Besides mastering the TV's remote control, he had also learned how to tap on the computer keyboard with his hoof. Google searches were his specialty. Laura had even noticed traces of slang creeping into his speech, which used to be so cultured and sophisticated. Now he took great glee in speaking like the teens he saw on television, dropping phrases such as "yeah, what*ever*" and "you go girlfriend" into conversations. Laura wasn't sure she liked it. His new street-talk just reminded her of how humanized he was becoming.

Flash sometimes seemed sad, especially when speaking of the fabulous land of Elysia where he had lived—a land of peace and incredible beauty, until the hostile

Troglodynes and their evil allies, the Odious Brotherhood of Wizards, swept through and war erupted.

Dusk was falling as the three friends paid their admission at the fairground gates and strolled across the expanse of grass towards the grandstands. The group stopped at a busy snack shack to buy a large bucket of popcorn, as much for Flash as any of them, as he loved the fluffy kernels.

Laura, Krissy and Todd staked out a place on the lawn away from the crowded grandstand, where there was less chance that Flash would be seen. He often couldn't be trusted to stay quiet and hidden when he became excited, squealing and flapping his wings even though he had promised to behave.

A local soft rock group finished their set and it was time for High Octane to take the stage. Laura always felt the strangest mixture of pride and embarrassment when watching her parents perform. This night was no exception—but in the end, pride won out.

The band was, as Tom would later describe them, "Locked up tight and smokin'." CeeCee's voice was soft and sultry for the old jazz numbers, fresh and vibrant for the top-40 songs. The horn section was electrifying and the outdoor venue made the seven-piece group sound large and spectacular. The crowd was loving it, including

Flash, whose head was bobbing up and down in time to the music. "That's *sick*," he said happily. "It's *bangin'!*" The kids laughed.

High Octane's set drew to a close to enthusiastic applause and shouts for more. They obliged with another song, Sister Sledge's old-school funk tune "We Are Family," which was met with roars of approval and got the entire crowd on its feet, dancing.

When the set was over, High Octane quickly cleared the stage to allow the feature group to set up. An hour and three encores later, the show wrapped up and the crowd began to slowly disperse. The girls and Todd were heading toward the fairground exit when Laura suddenly laughed.

"Hey Todd, do you realize that the last time we were here, you were chasing Flash around with a fishing net, trying to kidnap him?"

Todd looked embarrassed, but managed a crooked smile. "You guys are never going to let me forget that, are you?"

"Nuh-*uhh*," came a muffled voice from Laura's backpack.

The kids walked down the quiet streets, heading through a part of town where the homes were smaller and older. The girls knew Todd often dreaded going home, especially on the weekends when his father's drinking reached epic proportions.

As if he heard their thoughts, Todd suddenly said, "He used to be a great guy, you know, my dad."

Laura and Krissy glanced at Todd with interest. He rarely spoke about his father, as if dealing with him in conversation was as uncomfortable as facing him in person.

He continued. "When I was a little kid we went fishing all the time, even school nights when the weather was good. He'd always take me to Dairy Queen afterward for a cone. The chocolate-dipped kind. He used to take me to football games, too. Then he got laid off at the plant— him and a hundred other people—and things just started to tank after that. Mom left and we lost the house and now we live in that dump."

His pace had slowed, and his shoulders drooped. "He used to be such a sharp dresser, and he could really dance, too. Not as good as those "Dancing With The Stars" guys, but pretty good. Some nights I would catch Mom and him slow dancing in the living room after they thought I was asleep." He came to a halt. "I used to see them kissing and tickling each other when they thought I wasn't looking, too. It used to kinda gross me out," he said, his voice catching in his throat, "and they fought a lot, even back in those days, but you know, I'd take it all back in a heartbeat."

The girls were shaken by his candor. Todd stood in the harsh shadows of the streetlights, tears glistening in his eyes and staining his cheeks. He suddenly wiped the back of his hand angrily against his face, wicking away the offending tears, and strode off along the sidewalk.

Nobody spoke until they paused in front of Todd's rundown cottage. "Maybe he's already asleep," Krissy, always the optimist, said hopefully.

"Yeah," Todd replied. The trio briefly touched thumbs, their form of secret "handshake" since forming the Triad. With a sigh and slumped shoulders, Todd headed up the walkway.

Before he reached the door it was wrenched open. A figure stood, backlit by the dim interior light.

"Where the hell have you been?" came a gruff, slightly slurry voice.

Todd hesitated only a second before brushing past his father without answering.

"Hey! Don't you ignore, me, you little—" Mr. Williams roared. He swung an arm at the boy as he retreated into the house, missed, lost his balance and stumbled backwards across the porch.

The girls held their breath from their vantage point

on the sidewalk as he careened into the house. The door slammed shut, but the yelling, now muffled, continued.

Laura grabbed Krissy's arm. "Let's get out of here," she hissed.

The girls discussed their friend's plight on their way back to the Connor house. "I wish there was something we could do to straighten Todd's dad out," Laura said, shifting the backpack. "I can't imagine what it's like to have a parent who's always raggin' on you and whacking you around."

"Me neither," Krissy agreed. "My parents can be pretty lame sometimes, but they would never do anything to hurt me. Todd needs help before things get any worse."

"Except he doesn't seem to want any help," Laura said sadly. "I'm so scared that something really awful is going to happen to him."

The girls walked the rest of the way home in silence.

Chapter 3

Laura was flying.

She was sitting astride Flash's silky back, anchored by a hank of mane gripped firmly in her right hand. His wings made a soft, swooshing sound as he rose above the trees. Ahead of them lay purple mountains silhouetted against a rose-coloured sunset. Below, the tops of large maples gave way to huge old evergreens. Well-worn dirt paths were visible between the branches. Ponds and small lakes dotted the landscape for as far as she could see. Was Flash full-sized, or was she tiny? Laura wasn't sure.

The terrain began to change as they approached the mountains. Strange, tall mesas surrounded by steep sandstone cliffs jutted up. A thin ribbon of river snaked through the formations, reflecting the pinks and golds of the setting sun. Laura could see large birds floating lazily in the updrafts far below them. Were they eagles, condors...or pterodactyls?

She spotted a lone figure standing on top of the tallest mesa. He was ancient and wizened, and dressed in dark robes that seemed alive with movement, even though there was little wind. He raised a bony forefinger to the girl and the winged horse. There was a brief, intense light, a sound like distant thunder, and suddenly they were falling...falling...

Laura awoke violently, her heart thudding. She lay very still, eyes blinking rapidly in the dark. The dream had felt so real; the sensation of the air pushing against her as they flew, and the terrifying fall from the sky.

Laura turned her head towards the closet where Flash curled up every night. The faintest snoring told her that the little winged horse was fast asleep.

The wizard in the dream—had it been Malvenom, the same evil sorcerer who had cast a spell on Flash so many centuries ago? Laura tried to remember every detail. His long hair had been a deep red, the colour of dried blood, and there were two white streaks beginning at his temples which swept back along its entire length. The hand he had raised to her had long, yellow nails, and there was something else—a ring, a huge purple stone glittering on his index finger, the same finger with which he had knocked her out of the sky. Laura had seen a tanzanite ring in a jewelry store once. The wizard's gemstone resembled that, only his was a hundred times larger.

She shivered. An uneasy feeling remained. She felt that the dream was a premonition, a warning that Flash was somehow in danger. But how, and why?

She drifted back into a restless sleep.

~ ~ ~

The following morning, Laura rode her bike to Banbury Cross Stables to put in a few hours of barn chores. Summer vacation was nearly over, and Mrs. Leeds had suggested that Laura work only on Saturdays during the school year, providing she kept her grades up. Laura had originally been hired to replace the farm's regular employee, Sarah, who had broken her leg in a riding accident at the beginning of the summer. Even though Sarah was now fully recovered, Mrs. Leeds had asked Laura to stay on as well. She enjoyed the young girl's effort and enthusiasm, as well as her thirst for knowledge.

Laura could hardly pedal fast enough to get to the barn. She was excited to see the foal again, and chattered non-stop to Flash, who was listening intently from her backpack, head poking out, mane swept back in the breeze.

"You've gotta see him, Flash. He's adorable! So tiny, well, still lots bigger than you, though. I think Mrs. Leeds is naming him Spanish Bay. That one was my idea. He'll need a barn name, too. What do you think of Chico? That means "boy" in Spanish. I wonder if I'll be allowed to ride him when he's older..."

And so it went until the two of them wheeled into the driveway at the farm.

Mrs. Leeds greeted Laura at the door to the barn.

"Oh, good, I'm so glad you're here," she said. "I really need to slip out to the feed store and tack repair shop. Would you mind checking on Alba and the foal now and then while I'm gone?"

"Just try and stop me," Laura replied with a laugh. The farm owner briefly outlined Laura's duties for the day before heading out in the farm truck to run her errands.

Laura immediately released Flash from the backpack. "Come on—let's go and see the baby before Sarah or any of the boarders get here," she said. He lifted gracefully into the air and fluttered quietly behind her as she half-walked, half-trotted along the aisle to the foaling stall.

Laura eased slowly in front of the stall door to avoid startling Alba. The mare was near the back of the stall, standing protectively over the dark form of her sleeping foal. "Hi, sweetie," Laura whispered. Alba, true to her nature, pinned her ears and lifted her muzzle towards the girl, baring her teeth. Laura thought that if the mare could have snarled like a dog, she would have.

Over Laura's left shoulder, Flash levitated himself into view. Alba's demeanor immediately changed; her ears pricked forward with interest and the look in her eyes softened. Flash began chattering to her in his half-horse, half-human language that fascinated Laura. Alba murmured in response, nodding her head gently. To Laura's surprise, the usually unfriendly mare made her way carefully to the front of the stall and touched noses with Flash, who was now balanced precariously on the top of the dutch door.

Laura was astounded. She had never seen Alba make anything but aggressive gestures towards humans and the other horses at the stable, and yet here she was, making nice with Flash.

"What in the world did you say to her?" Laura asked in a hushed voice. "She hates *everyone*."

"Well," Flash replied, his voice remaining in the same, soothing lilt he had used with the mare, "I told her how beautiful her boy-horse was, and how I hoped he would grow up to be as fine and strong a horse as she." He winked. "I like mares."

A car door slammed in the parking lot. Laura did not

even have to tell Flash to hide; he was already gone.

As the boarders began to arrive to school their horses, Laura busied herself cleaning stalls. Gabrielle and Kerry-Lynn greeted her as they cross-tied their horses, but they were soon running breathlessly down to the foaling stall once Laura told them the news of the birth.

Mrs. Leeds arrived a short time later and Laura helped her unload the supplies. She had certainly toned up her muscles this summer with all the physical work, although she still had to move the heavy bags of grain in a wheelbarrow instead of hoisting them over her shoulder like Mrs. Leeds.

"I thought I'd turn mom and baby out in the round pen for a little while," Mrs. Leeds said when Laura was done her chores. "Want to stick around and watch?"

Laura thought that was a super idea and stood guard in the aisle while Mrs. Leeds led Alba out of her stall. The mare whickered anxiously and kept looking back to make sure her foal was following. The foal, on much less shaky legs than the day before, hesitated a moment at the stall door, then leaped into the aisle, slipping on the concrete and running into Laura. She instinctively steadied him with her hands and he clattered off after his dam.

With the pair safely in the round pen, Laura and Mrs. Leeds watched their antics with both pleasure and apprehension. Alba was glad to be outside after being cooped up in the barn and took off at a gallop around the pen with her little dark shadow trying to keep up. He was amazingly fast on his new legs, but the watchers were relieved when Alba finally pulled up, blowing hard. The foal continued to ricochet off the mare and the vinyl fencing, leaping and crow-hopping as if each limb was controlled by a different brain. His attempts at bucking were especially hilarious. Laura thought she had never seen a better display of "I'm so glad to be alive" in her life.

Chapter 4

Pedalling back to town along the tree-lined country roads, Laura gazed a bit wistfully at the trees that were showing signs they would soon be brilliant with autumn colours. The summer had raced by so fast. It seemed like just yesterday that she had celebrated her birthday with Krissy and Todd by having brunch, taking in a movie and enjoying an afternoon at the beach. That was nearly seven weeks ago! She sighed.

"What's the matter, toots?" came Flash's voice from behind her. He had watched some old gangster movies one rainy day when nobody was home.

"Oh, nothing," Laura replied. "It's just that I'm always a little bit sad at the end of the summer. I'm not sure why — there's lots of cool stuff to do in the fall, too. Going back to school and seeing everyone again, and playing soccer and watching the senior boys' football games, and the new shows on TV, and Thanksgiving and stuff..."

Flash was about to ask what a Thanks Giving was when they rounded the corner onto the road which bordered Turtle Creek. "Oh!" he said excitedly. "May I?"

Laura checked around her to make sure there were no cars coming, then said, "Go for it!"

With a swoosh, Flash launched himself out of the backpack and glided toward the river, where he levelled out a few feet over the water, wings fully outspread. He looked down at his reflection as he skimmed above the surface, safely hidden from view by the thick brush along the riverbank. Laura smiled as she caught a glimpse of her little companion. It was rare for him to be able to fly freely during daylight hours.

A great blue heron, startled from feeding in the shallows, launched itself into flight, looking like a large prehistoric animal. Flash was delighted to have a flying partner, but the panicked bird soon veered away from the river.

Back in town and safely out of sight again in the backpack, Flash lay low until Laura had put her bike back in the shed and was upstairs in her room. He clip-clopped into the closet, where Laura poured a handful of sweet feed she had pilfered from the barn into his bowl.

While he ate, Laura slipped into the bathroom, stripped off her sweaty, grimy clothes and ran a hot shower. She and Krissy had made plans to shop for school supplies that afternoon in the city, as her friend's mother had offered to take them to the mall. They had invited Todd along; he had seemed reluctant at first, and Laura suspected it was because he had no money for school supplies or anything else, but in the end he had agreed to come.

Before she left, Laura made sure that Flash had fresh water and a pile of carefully dried grass clippings from the back yard. She had read that fresh lawn cuttings could cause colic if fed to horses, and always tried her best not to feed him anything that might make him unwell. The very thought of him falling ill made her panicky. What would she do if he got sick, or badly hurt—or worse? It was so important to keep him a secret, yet she had no idea what to do if he needed veterinary care. "I guess we'll jump off that bridge when we get to it," she said aloud.

"Mwffft?" Flash asked through a mouthful of grass, looking at her quizzically.

Laura ruffled the silvery mane behind his ears, told him to behave, and left.

~ ~ ~

At two-fifteen, Laura and Krissy were still waiting impatiently for Todd to arrive so that they could head to the city. Mrs. Martineau was getting annoyed. "I'm sorry, girls, but I'd really like to get going," she said, looking at her watch.

"Just a couple more minutes, Mom," Krissy begged. It was not like Todd to be this late. He was usually the one who showed up ten minutes early for everything.

But as the minutes dragged by, it became apparent that Todd was not coming. Reluctantly, the girls climbed into the Martineau's SUV. "Maybe he's changed his mind 'cause he doesn't have any money," Krissy said, scanning the street behind them one last time as the van pulled away.

"Yeah, you're probably right," Laura muttered. *I hope that's the only reason,* she thought grimly.

In a whirlwind two-hour shopping frenzy, the girls stocked up on everything imaginable for the new school year. They each bought a new pair of jeans, a couple of sweaters and new running shoes. Laura was so proud to be able to pay for all her purchases with money she had made working at Banbury Cross. Her parents worked hard to make sure she had everything she needed, but she knew from experience that their music gigs would become more infrequent after the busy Christmas season, and money would become tighter until the spring wedding receptions were booked. Laura was glad she could help—it made her feel very grown-up.

Almost as an afterthought on their way out of the mall, Laura slipped back into a discount store and purchased another package of lined paper, a couple of binders and some pens. She also chose a nice set of coloured pencils and a pad of drawing paper. "For Todd," she said, seeing Krissy's quizzical look. "He needs to have *something* for school. He's a really good artist, too, you know. You should see the monsters and fantasy characters he draws. I'll just tell him that I bought way more stuff than I need."

Back at the Connor home, Laura and Krissy dropped their bags on the bench in the front hallway. Sounds of the band practicing wafted up the stairs from the basement studio. "I'll have to wait until the rehearsal's over to ask Mom if you can sleep over," Laura said. "In the meantime, let's go upstairs and try on our new clothes."

Flash was allowed to sniff and paw through the girls' bags of clothing and school supplies. Laura had bought some cheap sparkly silver nail polish for his hooves. "I'll paint some on you later," Laura promised. "But now, go to your room." She pointed to the closet. Flash snorted and trotted in, tail swinging. Krissy closed the door behind him.

"You're right," she said. "It would definitely be weird to try on clothes in front of him. Maybe if he was a girl horse I wouldn't mind so much."

The girls scampered downstairs just as the band was packing up to leave. Laura high-fived the guys on her way along the hallway to the kitchen, where her mother was starting to put dinner together.

"What's up?" Laura asked. "You guys hardly ever rehearse on Saturdays."

"We have to play a bat mitzvah party tomorrow, and we wanted to work on a couple of new tunes," her mother answered, popping a cherry tomato into her mouth before dumping the contents of the container into a wooden salad bowl.

"What on earth is a bat-what-zit?" Krissy asked.

"Well," Mrs. Connor replied, "In the Jewish faith, when a boy turns thirteen, his parents hold a big party for him called a 'bar mitzvah.' It celebrates his change from a boy to a man." Laura thought of the disgusting boys in her class who still thought boogers were funny and decided that Jewish boys must mature faster. Her mother continued. "When a girl comes of age at twelve, she is given a bat mitzvah. It's not just a party; there is a religious ceremony first and the child has to recite it all in Hebrew, which takes weeks to learn.

"The parties can be really spectacular, though. We were hired to play a huge bar mitzvah in Michigan last year and that event cost the parents well over $100,000." The girls gasped. "High Octane played mainly for the adult guests. The kids were in a separate ballroom with a DJ, dance instructors, giant video screens, a cartoonist, videographers, food stations, a chocolate fountain, a sundae bar—you name it."

Krissy's mouth hung open. "Wow! And to think all I got was a new pair of Crocs and a gift card to Mickey D's for *my* twelfth birthday!"

Laura changed the subject. "Mom, did Todd call here today?"

"No, hon, I though he was with you."

"He never showed up," Laura said, concern in her voice. "I'm getting kind of worried."

"Give him a call, then," her mother suggested.

Laura picked up the phone and punched in Todd's number. She silently held the receiver to her ear, letting it ring many times. Nobody picked up.

Laura and Krissy helped clean up after dinner so that the Connors could leave for their local bar gig. It was Labour Day weekend and the bar owners were expecting a standing-room-only crowd as the locals and cottagers enjoyed the last long weekend of the summer.

After feeding Flash and letting him out for a spin in the near-darkness of the back yard, Laura made good her promise and carefully painted his hooves with the glitter nail polish. He was delighted with the result, lifting each of his feet in turn and admiring them from every angle in front of the dresser mirror.

The girls tried calling Todd several more times during the evening.

There was still no answer.

Chapter 5

Laura and Krissy stayed up very late solving all the world's problems and speculating about what the coming school year would bring. "I hope I don't have Tanya Billings in any of my classes," Laura said fervently. "She was *so* mean to me last year. I don't know what her problem is. I try to stay out of her way, but she's always sneaking up behind me and calling me 'horse butt lover' and hip-checking me into the lockers."

"I heard that she broke Melissa Penski's arm over the summer," Krissy whispered excitedly. "Her parents were going to press charges, but Tanya said it was an accident, that Melissa just tripped and fell down the library steps."

Laura admitted to Krissy that she had even done some on-line research about bullying and how to prevent it. "I just wanted to know if I was doing something wrong," she told Krissy. "But I'm not. Nobody asks to be bullied. The best advice I found was to just stay out of the person's way, and keep friends around you all the time. I even read about some poor girl who tried to burn off her freckles because the other kids teased her about them so much." Her hand trailed absently to the faint smattering across her own nose. "I like my freckles."

And so they talked into the night, about favourite teachers and TV shows and music and boys. They seemed to be talking about boys a lot lately, Laura reflected just before she fell asleep. But the only boy who really concerned her right now was Todd. Where *was* he?

~ ~ ~

The house was unusually quiet when Laura awoke the following morning. She had slept through her parents clattering in with their gear long after two a.m. Even Flash, usually awake with the birds, was still curled up in his closet bed.

"Krissy!" Laura ordered, poking her friend's shoulder. "Pssst! Get up!"

Krissy responded by pulling the sheet up over her crazy mop of brown hair. "Go 'way," she mumbled from under the covers.

"Come *on*," Laura insisted, yanking the bedsheets down and off with one tug.

Krissy blinked sleepily. "What's the hurry?"

Laura tossed her friend's overnight bag on the bed. "Get dressed. We'll grab some breakfast and get out of here while my parents are still asleep." She ran a brush through her own tangled hair. "We're going over to Todd's house."

"Ugh." Krissy was clearly not thrilled by the idea. "That place creeps me out." She reluctantly dug through her bag for clean clothes while Laura headed for the door. "Bring Flash with you," she said over her shoulder as she left the room.

By the time Krissy tiptoed downstairs, Laura had juice and toasted bagel halves slathered with cream cheese waiting on the kitchen table. Flash's elegant little head peeked out of the backpack, his normally sleek silver mane an unruly mess. Laura laughed at the sight. "What's up with us this morning?" she giggled. "We all look like we've been dragged through a knothole backwards!"

She left her parents a note outlining their plans. As the girls walked through the quiet neighbourhood, Laura could almost feel the summer ending. The air was very cool, not like the muggy mornings only a few weeks earlier. It even smelled different somehow, like fallen leaves and wet earth and wood smoke.

They arrived in front of the ramshackle cottage where Todd lived with his father. There were no signs of life. Laura took a deep breath and silently agreed with Krissy's opinion that this place was both scary and creepy. *Screepy.* She steeled her nerve and strode up the crumbling concrete walk. Hesitating only a moment, she rapped loudly on the door.

Nothing. She was just about to knock again when there was a muffled crash from inside, followed by a curse. A moment later the door was wrenched open and Mr. Williams stood shakily in the entrance. He looked awful. He was sporting several days' growth of beard and smelled like cigarettes, even from where Laura was standing six feet away. His eyes were bloodshot, but it was his hair that really caught Laura's attention. It was squashed flat on one side of his head and spiked crazily into the air on the other. *Like Flash's mane this morning*, Laura noted.

"Whaddya want?" Mr. Williams asked gruffly. This was immediately followed by a fit of coughing.

"We're looking for Todd," Laura said when he had recovered. "Is he here?"

Mr. Williams smirked uneasily and looked down his nose at the girl on his steps. He pulled a crumpled pack of cigarettes from his shirt pocket and lit one. He inhaled deeply, then exhaled a long stream of foul smoke. "Nope," he said finally.

"Would you happen to know where he is?" Laura was trying to be as polite as possible, even though every instinct was telling her to scream and run away.

"Nope," he repeated again, then coughed and spat. "Who the heck are you, anyway? Are you his little girlfriend? You seem kinda young."

Now Laura was indignant. "I'm not his girlfriend!" She'd had enough and this was clearly going nowhere. She turned and stormed off down the weedy walkway.

"Listen, Missy!" Mr. Williams called after her, then he shook his head and waved a dismissive hand at her departing back. "Gaaah," he muttered, then pulled back into the cottage and slammed the door.

"Yikes," Krissy said when her friend returned to the sidewalk.

"What a vile man," Flash remarked with disgust from his hiding place.

"What now?" Krissy asked. "Can we please at least get out of this neighbourhood? It gives me the willies."

"Where else could Todd be?" Laura mused as they walked. "Does he have any friends, I mean, besides us?"

"I never saw him hang with anybody at school," Krissy noted. "He was always a loner. That's one of the reasons we thought he was weird, remember?"

The girls' aimless wandering had brought them to a small public campground by the river. There were a few families enjoying the pleasant weekend weather, cooking breakfast on camp stoves and open fires outside their tents and campers. The girls found a secluded spot at the far end of the park and released Flash to scamper and graze.

Laura never tired of watching her little Pegasus play. He was so delicate and graceful, yet so strong, especially when his powerful wings lifted him off the grass to swoop and soar. As the early morning sun glinted off his silvery coat, Laura was slightly shocked to see his ribs clearly outlined against the skin along his sides. She had never noticed them before, in fact, he had always seemed in good flesh. *Maybe it's just the way the light is hitting him,* she thought uneasily. Still, she made a mental note to try to encourage him to eat more.

Flash took flight and quickly flew out over the water and farther upriver before Laura could call him back. He was only gone a few moments before darting back over the low river brush and circling Laura frantically.

"You had better come and see this," he said urgently, then headed back up the river.

The girls, curious and a little frightened by the

concern in Flash's voice, took off at a dead run. They followed a winding, overgrown path, their legs getting scratched mercilessly by brambles and prickle bushes. They burst into a small clearing in the trees and skidded to a halt. Krissy piled into the back of Laura, who yelped.

In the long grass stood a primitive lean-to shelter made of long branches braced against a low tree limb and covered by a dingy blanket. And sitting in front of it in the cold morning sun, his right arm wrapped in a crude bandage, was Todd.

Todd didn't seem to notice the girls right away, as his attention was focussed on idly digging a stick into the ground with his left hand. When Flash landed in front of him he looked up, startled. As his gaze fell on the girls, who were clinging to each other, he managed a brief, crooked smile, then went back to poking in the dirt.

"Hi," he said weakly.

"What are you doing here?" Laura asked, taking hesitant steps towards him. "We've been worried sick, you know—" She stopped. Her voice had a shrill, scolding tone, but that was not how she meant to sound. "Hey, are you okay?" she continued, her voice softening.

"Not really," he replied, shrugging.

"What happened?" Krissy asked. "We were at your house looking for you, but you weren't there, probably because you were here. Why are you here?"

Todd finally looked up at the girls. "My old man and I had a fight—a big one this time. He wants me to quit school and get a full-time job to help out with the bills, but I said no way. He told me I'm ... I'm useless in school anyway and I'm just taking up space, so I might as well quit."

Todd took a deep breath. "He started slappin' me around again, but this time I got in a few shots myself." He peered up through thick strands of black hair at the girls, who were now kneeling in front of him. "On my way down the front steps he shoved me really hard and I fell. I think I broke my wrist."

The girls exchanged glances, horrified. "But you have to go to the hospital!" Krissy cried.

"We'll take you," Laura chimed in.

Todd looked embarrassed. "Naaw, it'll be okay." But when he raised his arm to show how okay he really was, he winced.

Laura stood. "That's it. You're coming with us. I'll ask my mom to drive us. You can't live in the woods forever, Nature Boy." Her weak attempt at humour fell flat, but Todd slowly got to his feet and followed the girls back down the path.

Laura had forgotten about Flash, who had been

watching and listening from the top of the lean-to. He flew above the trio's heads and obediently slipped into the backpack when Krissy held it open for him. He was uncharacteristically quiet during the walk back home.

Laura's parents were shuffling sleepily around the kitchen with their morning coffees when the three kids burst through the back door. CeeCee and Tom listened intently while Laura breathlessly recounted Todd's story. Her parents' expressions of genuine concern made the boy squirm uneasily in his chair.

"May I look at that?" Mrs. Connor asked, indicating the bandaged wrist. Todd nodded and she gently unwound the dirty dishtowel serving as a support. Todd bit his lip and stared bravely ahead, but it was obvious he was in some pain. His swollen wrist was already bruising in ugly shades of purple.

Laura's mother found a tensor bandage in the medicine cabinet and wrapped it gently and not too tightly around Todd's wrist and forearm. "That will hold until we can get you to the clinic," CeeCee announced. Todd looked as though he was about to protest, then slumped back in his chair, sighing.

Half an hour later, Laura, her mother, Todd and Krissy were sitting in a crowded waiting room at the local walk-in clinic. As is usual for a holiday weekend, it was populated with weekend warriors who had fallen off their mountain bikes, or slipped on their docks, or wounded themselves with some power tool or other. There was even one red-faced man, Laura noticed, who seemed to have no eyebrows. "Barbeque lighting explosion, I'll bet," her mother whispered.

Todd was seen in turn by the busy but cheerful female doctor. His wrist, as it turned out, was not broken. "We call it a greenstick fracture," she explained. "Not a clean break, but just as painful." She expertly applied a stiff but lightweight removable cast to the injured wrist, and the four were dismissed.

But what now?

"You can't go back there," Krissy insisted. She couldn't even say "back home," for Todd's residence was far from homey. "You can stay at my house. My mom won't mind. We have a little spare room in the basement. You can sleep there."

"Naw, I couldn't," Todd said, flustered. "I'll just wait until Pops falls asleep tonight and sneak back in."

"You'll do no such thing!" Mrs. Connor cried. "I'll speak to the Martineaus and we'll get you set up there until we can sort this out. You know, we really should contact the Children's Aid Society, and the police. You can press charges—"

"*No!*" Todd's reaction was swift. "You think he's hot at me now? Imagine what he'd do to me if the cops showed up at the door."

CeeCee opened her mouth to argue, then gave up. "Just promise me you'll stay away for at least one more night." She looked at him intently. He dropped his gaze and said quietly, "Okay."

Krissy's mother and father listened to their daughter retell Todd's tale of woe, all the while interjecting comments such as "how awful" and "that's terrible" and "you poor thing." "Of course you can stay here as long as you like," Mrs. Martineau said. "Krissy, take down some clean bedding and open the window downstairs to air out that basement room a bit."

They invited Todd to take a shower, and he was happy to oblige. He closed the door to the tiny basement washroom, fiddled with the controls in the corner shower, and carefully slipped off his cast before he stepped into the steamy spray. Mrs. Martineau scooped up the clothes he had left outside the bathroom door and tossed them into the washing machine. She replaced them with an old pair of jeans and a t-shirt left behind by Krissy's brother, James, who was away at veterinary school. She walked back upstairs, shaking her head sadly. She hesitated for a moment in front of the phone in the kitchen, then picked it up and dialed.

Chapter 6

Within the hour, Krissy and Todd arrived at Laura's house and the three set about salvaging the rest of their day. The girls wanted to keep Todd distracted, so they suggested funny movies to rent, and activities such as going to the arcade, or playing World of Warcraft or Halo Reach, which their friend loved. Todd was unenthusiastic; the events of the past day had drained him physically and emotionally.

"I know—let's go visit the foal," Laura suggested. "My mom will drive us to the farm. He's so cute, Todd, you've got to see him."

Todd looked doubtful, but must have sensed the genuine excitement in Laura's voice. "Okay, I guess," he agreed.

CeeCee was happy to drop the kids off at the farm. "I've got some errands to run, so I'll be back in an hour or so," she said as Laura kissed her lightly on the cheek.

Talking in hushed tones, the three walked through the quiet barn and out to the small pen where Alba and her baby were enjoying the late summer day. Alba was dozing, her head low, tail swishing occasionally, standing guard over her foal, who was sprawled on the ground in a deep sleep.

"Awww," Krissy breathed. Alba's head snapped up immediately. She snorted and stamped a hoof, which woke her foal. He raised his head and stared at the visitors, then struggled to his feet, balancing awkwardly for a moment on his stilt-like legs. He nickered and nodded his head up and down, then plunged toward the onlookers in three ungainly bounds. The girls giggled and even Todd laughed at the foal's antics. Little Spanish Bay—Laura was certain the name was perfect for him—scampered sideways like a crab, made an attempt to rear, then approached the teenagers.

Three outstretched hands were presented for the foal to sniff. He snuffled each one in turn, then gently lipped Todd's fingers. "Too cool," Todd said, smiling.

"You won't be able to let him chew on your fingers for much longer," said a voice behind them. They turned to find Mrs. Leeds, armed with a cotton lead shank. "Once colts realize they have teeth, they love to use them."

Laura introduced Todd to the farm owner, who glanced at the cast on his arm, but did not comment on it. "So nice to meet a friend of Laura's," she said warmly, and then, turning to Laura, "I was just about to bring momma and baby inside. You kids could get behind him and help herd him in."

"Why don't you just lead him in?" Krissy asked.

"Well, dear, he's not been halter-broken or trained to lead yet. That will come soon enough. For now, I just want him to have fun being a baby."

Mrs. Leeds opened the door and the four of them walked into the small turnout pen. Alba immediately pinned her ears and put on her ugly get-away-from-my-baby face. Mrs. Leeds calmly snapped the lead line onto the mare's halter and led her toward the barn door. Alba looked back anxiously at her foal, who had retreated to the farthest corner of the paddock, and whinnied nervously. The foal replied and scampered forward to join his dam. The kids formed a V behind the pair, moving forward to encourage the foal when he stopped at the entrance to the barn, unsure about stepping from the light into the darkness.

Laura clucked gently and said "Get up, little guy," as

he danced in the doorway. She placed her hands on his rump, and was again amazed at the thick softness of his coat. He was like a giant plush toy, she thought, as he trotted down the aisle after his dam to their stall.

With the mare and foal safely squared away, Laura showed Todd through the rest of the barn, stopping in front of the only other stall with an occupant, a large bay warmblood gelding with a kind face. "This is Dudley," she said. "He's inside today because he clipped himself at the last combined training event he was at, and his tendon is a bit warm, so Mrs. Leeds wants to keep him in for a couple of days."

Todd nodded, even though he had no idea what 'clipped' meant, or what a combined training event was. He didn't want to look dumb in front of the girls. Laura caught the brief look of doubt which crossed his face, then explained. "Sometimes, when horses are running and jumping, their hind hooves can strike the back of their front legs below the knees, where the tendons are, and hurt them. They usually wear tendon boots for protection, but accidents can still happen."

Their next stop was the feed room, where Laura showed Todd the various grain mixtures and special supplements the horses were fed. He seemed quite impressed. "I thought they just ate grass," he marvelled.

"When they were roaming the prairies free, yeah," said Krissy, who was beginning to fancy herself a horse expert after just a handful of trips to the barn. "But now they live indoors a lot of the time and are asked to work hard, so they need special food."

During a quick trip through the tack room, Todd was again overwhelmed by the array of saddles, bridles, blankets, bits and various leather straps, the purpose of which he could not imagine. The three then went outside to the paddocks to visit the rest of the Banbury Cross residents.

The four equines in the paddocks looked hopefully toward Laura and her companions. Laura laughed at their expressions. "Sorry guys," she called, "it's not dinnertime yet."

Todd met every horse in turn, petting each timidly on the muzzle. He was charmed by Smidge, the friendly little black pony, but decided that "the whitish one" was his favourite. "That's Phantom," Laura said, "and actually, he's called a grey."

Back in the barn, Mrs. Leeds approached the three. "I don't expect you to come in to work tomorrow," she said to Laura. "It's the last day of your summer vacation, so enjoy it. I'll work you like a slave again next weekend."

Laura inwardly breathed a sigh of relief. She loved her

job and couldn't wait to come to the barn to work and ride and just be with the horses, but she really did want to kick back and relax before school started.

The crunching of gravel in the driveway announced the return of Mrs. Connor, so after hasty goodbyes the three friends piled into the van and were soon on their way back home.

'Home' for Todd meant Krissy's basement, which is where the three of them ended up for the rest of the afternoon, playing Wii golf and tennis on the small TV and eating pizza rolls. Todd had to play left-handed, but he still trounced the girls game after game.

~ ~ ~

Laura slipped back home to rescue Flash, whom she was certain would be feeling cooped up and ignored. He was quick to make his feelings known. "Oh, will you grace me with your presence now, my cruel mistress?" he said sarcastically, flapping his wings and bowing deeply.

"I'm so sorry, Flash," Laura apologized. "We couldn't really take you to the hospital or even the barn today. I promise I'll make it up to you tomorrow. You can come back to Krissy's with me for a bit tonight. Oh, and I brought you a treat from the barn." From her pocket Laura produced a large handful of sweet feed and a couple of hay pellets. To a regular horse, an alfalfa nugget was barely a morsel, but tiny Flash looked like a dog gnawing happily on a bone. Once again, Laura grinned broadly at the sight of her beloved little flying horse.

Laura returned to Krissy's house with Flash and a few movie DVDs squirreled away in her backpack. Everyone was out on the back deck, enjoying the cool evening and the spectacular sunset. Laura greeted Krissy's parents and made enough small talk to be polite. Krissy and Todd eyed the backpack, shared a knowing glance with Laura and made their way towards the back door. "We're going to watch a couple of movies and hang," Krissy said over her shoulder as they thumped down the basement stairs.

Once they were settled and Flash was flitting cheerfully around the basement, exploring, Laura became serious. "I'm not sure what you're planning to do," she said to Todd, "you know, about your dad and all, but just remember that we're here for each other, always. We're the Turtle Creek Triad, right? The pact was sealed in blood, which makes it unbreakable forever."

"Yeah," Krissy agreed, leaning forward. "We've got your back."

There was a crash from the laundry room. "So sorry," came Flash's apologetic voice. "Won't happen again."

"You're right it won't happen again, 'cause whatever

you knocked down is broken now," Laura muttered. But the serious mood had been disrupted and the friends watched movies until they were all yawning. Laura sleepily gathered up Flash and trundled off home.

It was very late, so after kissing her parents goodnight, Laura splashed her face, brushed her teeth and fell exhausted into bed. She mulled the events of the day over in her mind, especially the questions about Todd's future, before she slipped into a deep sleep.

Chapter 7

The house was quiet. The digital clock on Laura's dresser glowed 1:13 as Flash crept as lightly as possible across the wooden floor of the bedroom. He rose gently into the air and passed soundlessly over the girl, whose deep and even breathing indicated that she was still sound asleep.

Satisfied, Flash glided over to the window sill, landing lightly. One of the panes was open to let in the sweet, cool night air. Deftly, Flash pushed his nose through a tear at the bottom of the screen—a tear he had created weeks ago with a sharp hoof. He had been restless one hot, moonless summer night and wanted to go flying under the cover of darkness. His escape hatch had so far gone unnoticed, and he had slipped outside many times since then to enjoy the rare freedom of soaring above the dark landscape.

This night, however, he had a special destination in mind. As he flew effortlessly over the silent and empty roadways, avoiding the powerlines and tall trees, Flash felt a thrill of excitement. He knew his mistress would never approve of what he was about to do, but he felt empowered anyway.

Minutes later, he landed on the window ledge outside Todd's house. Inside, the living room was lit by an eerie bluish light which flickered and cast strange shadows. Todd's father sat in a well-worn armchair in front of the television. He seemed engrossed in watching an old black-and-white western as he sat in the otherwise dark room. Empty beer bottles littered the side table, where an ashtray overflowed with cigarette butts.

It was easy for Flash to slip through the open, screenless window. He flew into the room and landed on top of the television set. He rose up and flapped his long wings. It still took Mr. Williams several moments to focus on the apparition.

"Good evening," Flash said loudly. "I think we need to have a talk."

The man blinked rapidly several times, then rubbed his eyes and leaned forward. "Who the hell are you?" he demanded.

"Who I am is not important," Flash said steadily. "Consider me a messenger. And the message I am delivering is this: under no circumstances are you to ever again harm your son, or speak to him in a hurtful manner, or there will be serious consequences."

Mr. Williams sat back, mouth agape.

"Todd is a good boy," Flash continued, his golden-eyed gaze unwavering. "He needs guidance from a caring, sober parent. It's time you pulled yourself together and became a real father." With that, he launched himself into the air and hovered in front of the awestruck man, who cringed in terror and threw his arms up in front of his face. "Leave me alone!" he cried, swatting at the intruder.

Flash easily avoided his flailing hands and moved away to a safer distance.

"If you ever harm Todd again, the authorities will become involved and you will be charged." Flash had learned this handy tidbit of information while watching Court TV.

"*Get out!*" Mr. Williams yelled. He picked up a nearby beer bottle and threw it at the winged monster which had invaded his living room. Flash neatly avoided the missile, which smashed noisily against the far wall. He decided it was time to beat a retreat, and swooped gracefully out the open window.

~ ~ ~

The last day of summer vacation. Laura, staring at the bedroom ceiling, felt that odd mixture of sadness and nervous anticipation which always seemed to overcome her on Labour Day. She sighed deeply and vowed that she would squeeze the most out of this day, starting right now.

She padded to the closet and poked her head inside. "Flash! Get up, sleepyhead."

She was greeted by the soft flapping of wings as Flash stretched, then trotted brightly out into the room. Laura picked him up to hug him, then wrinkled her nose and sniffed. "Yuck. You smell like cigarettes and...and *beer.*"

Flash hastily wriggled from her grasp and coasted over to the window seat. "Silly girl. Just your imagination, I'm sure." He changed the subject. "So, what are we doing today?"

"Let's get over to Krissy's and come up with a game plan." Laura shooed the little horse back into the closet again while she dressed, then tucked him into her backpack and scurried down the stairs to the kitchen.

"No time for breakfast—gotta run," she said to her mother, who was cradling a cup of coffee at the table. "I'll call you from Krissy's and let you know what we're doing." She pulled on her sneakers and was gone, screen door slamming in her wake.

Krissy opened the door in answer to Laura's impatient knocking. "Shhh," she scolded. "My mom and dad are still asleep. Todd too, I think. Come on, I'll make you some hot chocolate. Want a piece of toast?"

The girls were eating quietly when Todd emerged from the basement, still wearing his borrowed clothes. "Morning," he greeted the pair. He glanced at Flash, whose head was peeping out of the backpack. "Flash-*meister.* Flash-*arama.* How's it hangin'?" Flash batted his eyelashes and snorted in response.

Laura was relieved that Todd seemed to be in an upbeat mood. "We're trying to figure out what to do today. Any ideas?"

At Krissy's urging, Todd slid two pieces of bread into the toaster and joined the girls at the table with a steaming mug of hot chocolate.

The plan was formed. With Todd's injured wrist, fun stuff such as mini golf, beach volleyball or rock climbing at the rec centre were out of the question. The trio decided that a day at the zoo would be perfect. "Don't worry—it's my treat," Laura said before Todd could refuse. She knew he had no money for trips to the zoo. "I think I can talk my mom into driving us. She has a friend who lives near there and they could visit for a few hours."

Todd looked dubiously at his clothes. "I really need to go home and change," he said. Laura shook her head. "No way. You can't go near that place, or that man."

The tall boy laughed bitterly. "I have to go home *sometime*. I can't live in your basement forever, Krissy."

Laura chewed her lip thoughtfully. "I have an idea. Back in a sec." She went out onto the front steps, flipped open her cell phone and called home.

"It's all set," she said when she returned to the kitchen. "Mom and Dad will drive us over to your house. You can get your clothes or whatever and then we'll go to the zoo." She took a deep breath. "But here's the thing. Apparently, Krissy's mom called the Children's Aid Society yesterday and the family service workers are going to meet you at your place to talk to your dad. We all think you need to get out of there for a while, for real. It's not safe."

Todd flushed, embarrassed and angry. He opened his mouth to protest, but Laura interrupted. "No! This has gone on long enough. You're just—what did my mom call it?—"enabling" him by ignoring the problem and tiptoeing around, trying not to make him mad." Todd, looking completely defeated, said nothing.

~ ~ ~

The Connor van rolled to a stop in front of Todd's house. Todd had admitted to Laura that he was expecting

—and half-hoping—that his father wouldn't be there at all. But Mr. Williams *was* there, sitting out front on the top step, gripping a coffee mug. He looked up when his son got out of the van, then lowered his head.

"Pops," Todd said, coming to a halt at the bottom of the steps. His father rose wearily to his feet. The hand holding the mug was shaking badly, spilling drops of coffee onto the steps below.

"Son, I—" he began, then faltered. The two stared at each other for a moment, Todd defiantly, his father with a mix of shame and remorse in his eyes. "I'm so sorry for what I did," he continued, his voice rough with hangover and emotion. He glanced at Todd's bandaged wrist. "You okay?"

Todd shrugged. "It's all right. Just a fracture. It'll heal. Whadda you care, anyway?"

Mr. Williams sighed, shoulders sagging. "I know you don't believe me, but I do care. I know I've been a crappy father lately, but that's all going to change from now on."

Todd snorted. "I've heard *that* one before. How many times did you promise to quit drinking before Mom left? Five? Ten? Then you just fell off the wagon after a couple of days and it was business as usual. No wonder she bounced."

His father shook his head slowly. "No, something really

weird happened last night, made me realize I gotta stop boozing for good, before I go crazy." He leaned toward Todd and whispered, "I saw a monster."

Todd became interested. "What kind of monster?" he asked.

Mr. Williams glanced around to make sure no one else was within earshot. "A talking dragon!" he hissed.

"What?" Todd exclaimed, then laughed. "A *dragon?*"

"It was silver and no bigger than a seagull and had long wings and it told me I'd better be a good father to you," he said, "or else."

Todd's eyes widened. That was no dragon. He nearly laughed, but instead clapped a hand on his father's shoulder. "That's cool, whatever," he said. "Here's the thing, though," he added, his voice solemn. "If you want me to move back in, and you're serious about kicking the booze, we're going to do it the right way."

He gestured to the green sedan that had pulled up behind the Connor's van. Two people, a large man in a golf shirt and shorts and a thin woman in a business suit, approached the porch.

"Oh boy, here we go," said Laura from the back seat of the van, nose pressed against the window.

The four stood talking on the porch for a long time. There was a lot of hand gesturing, agitated conversation, and then papers being passed over to sign. Finally, Todd offered his hand and his father slowly accepted it, and with that handshake Mr. Williams began the long and bumpy road to recovery.

"I'm here to grab some clothes. We're going to the zoo." Todd said this as if going to the zoo was a regular occurrence, when in reality he had never been there in his life. "I'll be back later for the rest of my stuff."

"Sure, sure," his father said as Todd brushed past him and entered the house. The man turned and lifted his hand in a half-hearted wave at the departing family service workers and the group of people waiting anxiously in the van.

Todd was back with his friends minutes later. He was carrying a small suitcase and had a large garbage bag that clinked loudly as he placed it in the storage area behind the seats.

"What happened?" Laura and Krissy asked in unison.

"I guess I'm going to be staying with you for a while, Krissy," Todd said, a big grin spreading across his face.

"What?!" Krissy exclaimed. "That's awesome! Does my mom know?"

"It was your mom's idea," Todd replied. "The Children's Aid told your parents that they could provide temporary foster care for me if they wanted to. Those two family service workers are on their way over right now to meet with your folks and check out the living conditions."

Krissy was speechless. Todd continued, "Everything should be cool, as long as they don't have criminal records, or a grow-op in the basement, or guns in the house or anything like that." He laughed. "They don't, right?"

"*My* parents? Criminal records? Guns? Not likely!" Krissy retorted. "My parents are *soooo* straight."

"And what about your father?" Tom asked Todd. "Is he getting help?"

"If he wants me to move back in, he has to agree to certain conditions. No booze, and he has to attend counseling sessions twice a week. He agreed to go to Alcoholics Anonymous meetings, too, but who knows? He used to promise that all the time before Mom left, but this time I'll make sure he actually makes it to the AA meetings instead of sneaking off to Shakey's Roadhouse for a couple of cold ones. I'll drag him there myself if I have to." The tone of his voice left no doubt that he was serious about that.

Todd indicated the garbage bag in the back of the van. "Oh, by the way, that's all the booze that was in the house. I knew about his hiding places, too. He thinks he's so smart."

Laura was amazed at Todd's sudden take-charge

attitude. Maybe realizing that he wasn't alone, that there were people out there who wanted to help, had fueled him with new-found confidence and purpose. "They also told me about Alateen meetings in town I can go to. There will be other kids there I can talk to with messed-up or recovering parents."

He pulled a folded piece of paper out of his jeans pocket. "It says here the Children's Aid will meet with me and Pops regularly to see how he's making out, and to talk to me about, well, me—*my* health, *my* goals, *my* future." Todd put the paper back in his pocket. "No one's ever been interested in my future before," he said quietly.

Everyone was silent for a moment. Once the enormity of it all had sunk in, the van and its passengers began their trek towards the zoo.

~ ~ ~

After being dropped off at the front entrance, the three paid their admission and set off down the wide, tree-lined walkway. It was quite busy, but the park was so large that it didn't feel crowded at all. Strange smells filled the air, and from the distance came the squawks, cries and roars of the exotic residents.

Laura could feel Flash wriggling in the backpack. It was obvious that he, too, heard the exciting sounds and smelled the tantalizing odours, and was finding it all very exciting. He knew the rules, though, and had to be content with staring through the mesh and staying quiet.

"It was Flash," Todd said suddenly when they were on an isolated path near the giraffe habitat.

"What was?" Laura asked, her heart quickening the way it always did whenever his name was mentioned.

"It was Flash who went to my house last night and talked to my dad. His monster, as he called it. His dragon."

Laura stopped walking. "*What!?*"

Todd repeated what his father had told him. "It had to be Flash, see? Even in as bad a shape as my old man is, he's not crazy—at least, I'm pretty sure he's not. But let him think whatever he wants. He'll never tell anyone else, and at least it made him want to get help." He reached over and tapped gently on the backpack. "Thanks, dude."

Laura continued to walk, a bit unsteadily at first, as the enormity of Flash's latest act of disobedience sank in.

"I think Todd's right," Krissy said, trying to put a positive spin on the situation as usual. "Mr. Williams will never admit to anyone else that he saw a talking dragon in his living room."

Laura sighed. Flash had become very still in his carrier. "It's okay, Flash," she said over her shoulder. "It was a stupid thing to do, and it may not keep Mr. Williams clean and sober forever, but at least you got the ball rolling." Flash nickered, relieved.

The afternoon shadows were lengthening when the trio hopped back into the Connor family van for the ride home. This day, this entire summer, had been so exciting, and Laura was sad to see it coming to an end.

She looked out the window as Todd and Krissy described all the fabulous animals they had seen, arguing as to which were their favourites. What they didn't mention was how the chimpanzees had reacted when they caught sight of Flash peering out of the backpack. The shrieking, running and backflips were hilarious and the kids had laughed so hard they could barely breathe.

"Would you like to have dinner with us?" CeeCee offered before Laura could ask Todd the same question.

"No, but thanks anyway, Mrs. Connor," he said. "I think I'd better go home and see how my dad is making out, and grab some stuff for school tomorrow before I go back to Krissy's."

"Geez, Louise, I totally forgot!" Laura exclaimed. "I have a bunch of school supplies for you. Mom, can we swing by our place first?"

~ ~ ~

After dinner, Laura shook the dirt and horsehair out

of her backpack and filled it with her new school supplies. Flash watched with interest as she chose an outfit for her first day of grade eight. "Were there schools and teachers in Elysia?" Laura asked as she fussed in the closet.

"Teachers, yes, although we called them Masters and they taught us flying and fighting skills. Everything else we learned from our parents before we left home," he explained. "Reading, ancestry, even mathematics."

"So you were sort of home-schooled," Laura said. Flash had been staring intently at her with large, pleading eyes. She smiled. "Yes, you may come with me to school," she said, then held up a warning forefinger as his ears perked up, "but not tomorrow."

Flash's head drooped, knowing there would be no convincing his mistress once she had made up her mind.

Chapter 8

On Tuesday morning, Laura met up with Krissy and Todd for the walk to school. There were buses for the kids who lived out in the county, but the three friends lived within easy hiking distance.

They chattered excitedly about the classmates they hadn't seen all summer and the sports they wanted to join. Turning onto the road leading to the school, Laura glanced upwards and winced. There, draped conspicuously over the powerlines, were a pair of her running shoes. She wrinkled her nose in distaste at the memory of how they came to be in that precarious position.

It had been the last week of school in June. Laura was walking home alone—her constant companion Krissy was at a dentist appointment—when Tanya Billings had come up behind her and shoved her roughly.

"Hey, Laura the Loser, Connor the Goner, how's the stinky horse butt lover girl?" Tanya had laughed mockingly. "What, no little friend today?"

Laura's gym shoes, knotted by the laces and hanging over her backpack, had fallen to the ground. In an instant, Tanya snatched them up and, swinging them over her head like a lariat, threw them skyward as hard as she could. They settled gracefully over the wires, where they had remained all summer—a constant and embarrassing reminder of Laura's helplessness against Tanya's bullying.

Krissy followed her friend's gaze. "What a *bee*-otch," she spat. "I'd like to throw Tanya's shoes up over the wires—with her in them."

Laura laughed ruefully. Her friend was stocky and "built low to the ground" as her father often kidded, but she was also surprisingly strong and an excellent soccer and baseball player. The thought of Krissy launching the much larger Tanya into space made Laura smile. She took a last glance at the dangling runners. Time and Mother Nature would decide when the laces would finally break and the shoes would return to earth.

The morning became a blur of new classes, new teachers, and catching up with the other students about their summer adventures. Laura was glad they didn't have to write essays anymore about "What I Did On My Summer Vacation." She was pretty sure her story would rock the assignment.

Laura briefly saw Todd, who was coming off his lunch break, while she was on her way to math class. She was surprised but pleased to see that he was talking to a couple of other boys and a dark-haired girl on the high school side of the building. This was certainly an improvement over last year when, on the rare occasions Laura had noticed Todd at all, he was usually skulking in a corner by himself.

He looked up. She caught his attention through the fence and waved.

After school, the three friends walked home together and compared notes. "Do you believe it?" Krissy complained. "I've got homework already."

"I'm lucky—I've got a spare at the end of the day so I can get some of it done then," Laura announced.

Todd patted the rucksack over his shoulder. "Got some English and science but the good news is that the new art teacher is smokin' hot!"

Laura laughed and punched his arm. "Boys!" she said in mock disgust.

~ ~ ~

Flash was eager to hear about Laura's first day at school, and listened attentively as she told him the parts she thought he'd find interesting — her teachers, history class, gym, lunch. She even told him the running shoe story, and how they had come to decorate the powerlines.

Flash looked puzzled. "Why did you not stand up to this Tanya person?" he asked. "Was she brandishing a weapon?"

"No," Laura replied, looking down at her hands. "It's just that she's scary, at least, she scares me. You wouldn't understand."

Flash snorted. "You need to develop some backbone, young lady. Any mistress of mine must be a brave warrior."

They were interrupted by Mrs. Connor calling up the stairs, announcing that dinner was ready. "We'll talk about this later," Laura said, and headed down to the kitchen.

~ ~ ~

It was dark and still when a small winged figure again slipped out through the hole in the screen window and sailed down the quiet streets. He was not just flying for the joy of it on this cool evening. He was on another mission.

~ ~ ~

Laura awoke to the blatting of her alarm clock. She rolled over with a groan and slapped the snooze button, then snuggled back under the covers. Just five more minutes...

Her gaze through half-closed eyes focused on the wide window seat. There, weathered and beaten, were her old running shoes.

She sat up slowly, blinking. She rubbed her eyes. The shoes were still there.

Flash fluttered out of his closet bedroom and landed beside them on the sill. "Ta daa!" he crowed. He seemed very pleased with himself.

"*Flaaash...*" Laura said, her voice accusing. "What have you been up to?"

Flash flapped his wings noisily. "Let's just say that you never need to be embarrassed to walk down that street again."

Laura slid out of bed and went over to inspect the runners. They were in a sad state, and certainly beyond ever wearing again, but she ruffled Flash's mane anyway and said, "Thanks."

"You're quite welcome," he replied. "Now, when may I go to school with you?"

Laura discussed this dilemma with Krissy and Todd over the next couple of days. "I feel so sorry for him.

He's locked up in my room all day, unless my parents go out. He's so bored," she lamented, "and he seems to be losing weight for some reason. I hope it's not 'cause he's unhappy."

Eventually, the Turtle Creek Triad decided that they would get the first week of school behind them and, against their better judgment, sneak Flash to class on Monday.

Chapter 9

It seemed to Laura as though Saturday would never come. Grade 8 was proving to be a lot tougher than Grade 7—more homework, more assignments, more rules, less free time—in short, more work and less fun. She was looking forward to doing barn chores at Banbury Cross again. She missed the horses, especially the new foal, and wanted badly to ride.

Mrs. Leeds had suggested that Laura start at eight o'clock in the morning instead of seven, partly to allow the tired schoolgirl to sleep in a bit, and partly because the sun was rising later and the mornings were darker now. The Connor van rolled up the farm's driveway at eight sharp, and an eager Laura bounced out.

After a brief visit with Alba and little Spanish Bay (as

Mrs. Leeds had decided to name him after all), Laura set to mucking out the stalls. It felt so good to be doing something physical after sitting on her butt in class all week. She fairly flew through the chores, moving the horses from stall to field, shoveling and making many trips to the manure pile with the big wheelbarrow before adding the fresh new shavings to the bedding. She swept, filled water buckets and set the evening feed before finding Mrs. Leeds in the tack room. The farm owner laughed. "Judging by the big smile on your face, you've done the chores and are ready for your riding lesson."

Laura nodded happily and went out to the paddock to catch Morning Glory. With the mare safely secured in the crossties, the young student set about carefully grooming her chestnut coat, noting that the hair was already getting thicker in preparation for winter. The dust flew in little puffs from the dandy brush with every flick of her wrist. She ran her fingers through the mare's fine auburn tail to gently detangle it before using the plastic curry to comb it out. She picked out each hoof thoroughly, leaving a little heap of dirt and stones on the floor, before placing each foot solidly back on the concrete, and not on top of her own toes.

Tacked up and in the outdoor ring, Laura warmed up Glory for a few minutes until her instructor arrived. She hoped they were going to work over jumps again today. Mrs. Leeds had recently started schooling her over small cavaletti and little cross-poles, and although nervous at first, Laura was beginning to really enjoy it.

As hoped, after twenty minutes of exercises at the walk, trot and canter, Mrs. Leeds set up an easy jumping line of three ground poles to a small "X." Laura tried to remember everything she had been taught—pick up a nice working trot, let your eyes lead you around the turn, straighten a few strides before the first pole, get into your two-point position, legs on, hands soft and following, and ride forward. Sweet old Glory perked up as soon as she saw the ground poles and trotted smartly through them, then popped lightly over the crossrail and cantered away from the jump.

"Excellent!" cried Mrs. Leeds. "Make sure you move away from the fence in a straight line, ease back into a trot and continue, nice and balanced, around the corner. Don't let her fall in... that's better."

Laura's heart soared. Riding was so much fun!

Girl and horse repeated the exercise a few more times before Mrs. Leeds announced that the lesson was over. Laura wished she could ride all day, but at the age of eighteen, Glory was a bit of a creaky senior citizen who deserved to not be worked too hard.

After cooling the mare out, which took less time lately as the sticky humidity of the summer had given way to cooler days, Laura untacked her and brushed her off before returning her to her friends in the field. Glory whinnied at the sight of Psycho and trotted happily out to meet him. After an initial sniff and mareish squeal, Glory dropped to the ground and rolled with great enjoyment. She got slowly to her feet, her old joints complaining a bit, and shook lightly. Bits of dirt and grass stuck to her coat, mane and tail. Laura smiled and shook her head. After all her careful grooming, Glory now looked a mess.

~ ~ ~

There was still plenty of day left by the time Laura and her mother arrived back at home. "What are your plans, hon?" her mother asked, then continued without waiting for a reply, "Your dad and I have a recording session this afternoon, and then we've been invited out to dinner with some friends. Will you be okay?"

Laura nodded yes. "Recording? Are you guys finally cutting a CD?" She had always thought that High Octane was good enough to sell albums, but her parents seemed to have no desire to pursue that aspect of their music careers.

"No, sweetie, we're just playing backup for some young

rising star who needs an experienced studio band behind her." She pointed to the slight crow's feet around her eyes. "See that? That's experience." CeeCee laughed and headed off to change.

Flash was delighted with the news. "Oh, boy," he said, bouncing with excitement on Laura's bed. "We can watch TV and have Cheezies and I can fly outside when the sun goes down—"

"Like you don't fly around after dark now?" Laura finished. She suspected Flash enjoyed far more nocturnal flights than he admitted to.

Flash ignored her. "What's for dinner?"

Once her parents were gone, Laura went to the kitchen to fix Flash a special meal. On a small plate she arranged apple slices, carrot sticks, some bean sprouts and a handful of granola. As an afterthought, she tossed in a fresh brussels sprout from a bowl in the fridge. She inspected her culinary creation with satisfaction.

"Dinner, Your Highness," she said grandly as she positioned the plate on the bed with a flourish. Flash immediately set to eating, crunching and slurping while Laura looked on. When he got to the brussels sprout, he sniffed it with suspicion and rolled it with his hoof.

"Brussels sprout," Laura said. When Flash looked at her blankly, she added, "Like a baby cabbage." With some difficulty, Flash pinned it between his front hooves and took a bite. He chewed slowly, then spat out the soggy mess. "Blecch!" he said in disgust.

Laura howled with laughter. "My feelings exactly!" she gasped when she could finally speak.

Chapter 10

Sunday dawned grey and miserable, but Laura didn't mind. She pulled the covers up and snuggled into their warmth, grateful for the chance to sleep in. By ten o'clock she had roused herself, done her homework assignment, an essay on alternative energy, and was thinking about calling Krissy. Her parents had other plans for her, though. Her aunt and uncle and their two boys, Greg and Gordie, were coming to visit for the afternoon.

Laura sighed. The boys were both several years younger than her and were pretty rough around the edges. They still thought armpit farts were hilarious, for heaven's sake.

The afternoon crawled by. Laura was happy to see Aunt June and Uncle Rick, who brought her some My

Little Pony stickers for which she thanked them profusely, even though she had outgrown that phase of her horse-craziness years ago. Greg and Gordie seemed to spend most of their visit running and fighting. Laura followed her cousins around and watched them anxiously whenever they were in her room in case they discovered Flash's hiding place. She had a disturbing mental image of them finding Flash, gleefully grabbing him and then tearing him apart while fighting over him. She shivered at the thought. The boys, however, found her model horses and girly things boring and quickly lost interest in her room.

Thankfully, the Connor relatives did not stay for dinner, saying goodbye with promises to get together more often. Laura scampered upstairs to see if Krissy was on Facebook and spent some time before supper chatting with her friend and bemoaning the onslaught of rude little boys.

~ ~ ~

"It's Monday! Time for school! Get up!"

Flash was prancing with glee on the bedspread, trotting over Laura's prone body, his sharp hooves poking into her tummy and making her wince.

"Get off me," she growled. "Nobody is ever this happy on a Monday morning."

But Flash was not to be discouraged. "Let's go!" He regained his composure, smoothing his feathers and arching his elegant neck. "I am ready to observe what occurs at the education facility."

Laura showered and dressed quickly. She looked doubtfully at her backpack, which although quite large, was now going to have to do double duty carrying books *and* Flash. She took a small hand towel from the bathroom and folded it on top of her textbooks. At least it would offer a little bit of padding for her passenger.

After wolfing down a piece of toast, Laura ran upstairs to zip Flash into the bag. "Oh," she said. "Are you hungry? I'm sorry, I was in such a hurry..."

He shook his head. "No thank you. Actually, I'm feeling a bit off. Maybe it was something I ate. Probably that brussels sprout." He winked at her.

"Are you sure you want to do this today?" Laura asked, concerned. Until recently, Flash had always been the picture of health. She had even wondered if he might be immortal, but lately he had lost weight and seemed listless, which worried her.

"I'll be fine," he assured her.

"Just don't leave any turds in my backpack," Laura warned, half-serious. "It's hard enough convincing teachers that your dog ate your homework, let alone that it was pooped on by a small flying horse."

~ ~ ~

"How's the hitchhiker?" Krissy asked when they met up on the street.

"Like a little kid," Laura replied. "He's so excited, he's given himself a stomach ache."

Laura hoped that Flash wouldn't get bored during the day. There wasn't much about science or English that he would find very exciting, she suspected. But, true to his word, Flash remained quietly out of sight in the backpack, watching through the dark mesh.

At lunch break, Laura and Krissy went to the far corner of a small nearby park so that Flash could stretch his legs and nibble some grass. He seemed relieved to be out of the bag and immediately trotted into some thick bushes nearby. Laura still found this charming. The horses at the barn had no qualms about going to the bathroom anywhere, anytime. Heck, they'd poop on your head while you were picking out their rear hooves if you weren't careful. Yet Flash was always a gentleman and sought out privacy.

"Ohhh, that wasn't good," he remarked when he rejoined the girls.

"Still not feeling well?" Laura asked. She was starting

to get really worried about his health.

"No worries, really," he reassured her. To show just how fine he was, he dropped his head and started grazing.

The girls finished their sandwiches. Laura offered Flash a piece of her granola bar, which he ate without much enthusiasm. She poured some water into her thermos lid and he drank, which made her feel better.

"Tell you what, Flash," Laura said. "If you'd rather hang outside for the rest of my classes, that's okay. There's only phys ed, which will probably be on the track anyway, and math, which is a big bore. The only thing is, you have to stay on the roof or in the trees behind the school. I'll meet you behind Portable 3, which is kind of out of the way. I don't think anyone will see us there."

Flash seemed grateful for the change of plans. "That might be best," he agreed.

Later, Laura thought she saw his silvery forelock and tiny ears as he peeked over the edge of the school roof while she ran laps on the track. She smiled.

On the way back to the locker rooms, Laura passed Todd in the hallway. He was loping along on his way to class, but stopped to talk to her for a moment. She hadn't seen him much since school started, and was surprised at how badly she missed him. "Flash is going to meet us behind P3 after school. Meet us there and we can all walk home together."

"Sure," he said, smiling. Laura thought he looked good—really good, happier and more relaxed than she had ever seen him. He was still sporting a toned-down version of his old goth look for school ("Gotta keep 'em guessing" was his theory), but Laura had learned through their friendship that you couldn't label someone just based on their clothes or appearance or taste in music.

"How's your dad doing?" Laura asked.

"So far, so good," he replied. "I've been walking him over to the AA meetings three times a week. He seems pretty quiet, and sorta depressed, but he says the counseling is helping." He linked his index and middle fingers. "Fingers crossed."

"And how are *you* doing?" Laura asked. This question brought a shy smile to Todd's lips.

"I'm okay, no, better than okay," he said. "I went to my first Alateen meeting, and it blew me away. There are all kinds of kids there—rich kids, poor kids, in-between kids. And they're not all there because their parents are drunks. One guy has an older brother who drinks and then drives, so he's worried his big bro is going to die in a flaming wreck. And one of the girls is freaked out about her little sister 'cause she likes to party too hard." His voice lowered. "You know, I think about what would have happened if I'd never met you and Krissy—and Flash, of course. Where would I be now?"

Laura did not have an answer for him.

~ ~ ~

The afternoon dragged on, and when the final bell rang at three-fifteen, Laura slammed her books shut, vaulted from her chair and headed down the hallway at a dead run. She nearly ran into Krissy at the back doors of the school. A passing teacher glared at them both. "Slow down, ladies!" he admonished.

The pair sauntered as nonchalantly as possible toward P3, waiting for the student stragglers to finish filing out. They sidled toward the back of the small building, scanning the nearby trees for the tiny flying equine. "Flash!" Laura called when she was fairly certain there was no one within earshot. "Flash!"

"Well, what do we have here?" snarled a voice from behind them. "It's the stinky horse lover girl and her little friend. What are you two losers doing way over here?"

It was Tanya and her posse. Laura felt an uneasy feeling in the pit of her stomach.

"This is our turf after school," Tanya said threateningly. "You've either got a lotta guts, or you're too stupid to know better." The much larger girl moved toward Laura, who glanced wildly to either side, seeking an escape route. But their way was blocked by Tanya's entourage.

"Come on, let's see how tough you are," Tanya said, shoving Laura roughly. She fell hard onto the ground, landing on her backpack. For one panicked moment she thought she had squished Flash, then remembered that he was not in the bag.

"Get up, you wimp," Tanya yelled, "or I'll—"

"—or you'll what?" The deep voice cause the girls to spin around. It was Todd, doing his best to look menacing.

Tanya was struck speechless, but only for a moment. "Great, another frickin' freak," she spat. "Whadda you want, kindergoth boy? What's your name these days anyway—Razor? Or is it Toad? You want your ass kicked, too?"

But before Todd could answer, the most extraordinary thing happened. There was a loud *splat* as a large blob of disgusting, watery green goo landed on Tanya's head. It slid in thick rivers through her dark red hair and dripped onto her shoulders. Tanya gasped. "What the—"

"Eeeew, gross! What *is* that?" one of Tanya's friends screamed in horror.

Laura, who had spent all summer mucking out stalls, knew exactly what it was. She clamped a hand over her mouth to prevent herself from laughing out loud.

Tanya's hand flew up to her hair and grasped some of the smelly substance sliding off her head. She examined it with absolute terror in her eyes, then flung it away and took off running, shaking her head and shrieking pitiously. Her friends, confused now that their leader had left, trailed after her.

Suddenly, the portable's door burst open behind them.

"Just exactly what is going on out here!?"

It was one of the new teachers. Laura didn't have him for any of her classes, and wasn't even sure of his name—McFee or Macnee or something.

Mr. McSomething surveyed the startled faces before him. "I was just marking papers and I heard the commotion. Was that the Billings girl I saw running away?"

All three nodded mutely.

"Was she bothering you? I thought I heard her making threats. Word has it she has a reputation for being a bully."

Again three heads nodded.

"So, what made her run off?"

The teens exchanged glances.

"She got, uh, hit with a turd. From a bird," said Laura.

"A big bird," added Krissy.

"A *really* big bird, like maybe an eagle," finished Todd.

Mr. McSomething chewed his lip in thought for a moment. "I'll report this incident to the principal tomorrow. In the meantime, try to stay out of her way." With that, he spun and re-entered the portable, closing the door firmly behind him.

Flash soared off the roof and joined them. "You crazy little horse!" Laura whispered gleefully. "That was terrible, but it was *awesome!*"

"I told you I wasn't feeling well," Flash reminded her, then whinnied happily.

~ ~ ~

The next day, Tanya Billings was reprimanded by the principal, and given a stern warning to leave Laura Connor—and everyone else—alone or face suspension and possibly expulsion. Tanya's parents were also contacted, but as is so often the case they refused to believe the accusations leveled at their darling daughter, insisting she was just a "confident leader type" who was "misunderstood."

Nevertheless, things at school changed a lot after the Sky Turd incident, as the Turtle Creek Triad came to call it. Although Tanya and her gang would often point at Laura, Krissy and Todd and whisper among themselves, they never confronted them again. Laura also heard that Tanya and her friends had posted some untrue and unkind remarks about her on their Facebook pages, but she really didn't care all that much. It would all be forgotten someday. They were leaving her alone, and that was enough for now.

She had no idea that the next challenge she would face would make Tanya Billings seem extremely unimportant.

Chapter 11

The next few weeks flew by. Todd and his father seemed to have reached an uneasy truce, but although Mr. Williams had been attending Alcoholics Anonymous meetings, Todd did not trust him completely and insisted he escort him there. Then one day he received a call from his father's counselor saying that he had missed an appointment. Todd walked over to his house to find his father sitting in the back yard with a six-pack. They had a terrible fight, according to Todd, but the next day Mr. Williams went to his AA meeting—sober.

It was all starting to take a toll on Todd, who worried, was incredibly angry at his father, and at times even felt responsible for his dad's drinking somehow. The Alateen meetings helped, for there he could vent his fears and frustrations with other teens experiencing the same problems.

"They tell me it's not my fault," Todd told Laura one day as they walked home from school. "At the meetings they say that my dad is the only one who can decide to not drink. There's nothing I can do or say to make him quit. And the worse part is, about half of all alcoholics who quit will drink again within six months to a year." He sighed. "My dad didn't even make it six weeks."

Laura felt fairly useless, as she had no experience with alcoholism whatsoever and no advice to give. The strangest thing that had ever happened at her home was when her dad had enjoyed a few too many mojitos at his 40th birthday barbeque, got extremely happy and loud for a bit, then passed out in the peony bushes in the back yard. Her mother took great glee in teasing him about that.

~ ~ ~

Laura signed up for the soccer team and tried to take Flash to school once in a while to ease his boredom. She worked at the stable on Saturdays, and was continually amazed at how quickly little Spanish Bay was growing.

Flash's health, however, was becoming a huge concern. Some days he seemed fine—his usual bright and fun-loving self—while at other times he seemed depressed and had no appetite. He continued to lose weight. Lately, the bad days were outnumbering the good and Laura was becoming increasingly worried.

She went online and looked up "horse diseases." She was pretty sure he didn't have West Nile or worms or strangles. His symptoms seemed more like frequent bouts of colic. But what was causing them?

Laura carefully made a list of everything Flash ate. He snacked on breakfast cereal sometimes, but not the sugar-coated kind, and loved granola bars, apples, carrots and other fresh veggies. She had planted some "indoor" grass for him to nibble on, and whenever no one was around, he was allowed into the back yard to graze. She even clipped and carefully dried the grass from the yard so he could have it to snack on whenever he was hungry. She had no idea what was making him ill.

Just before Thanksgiving, the situation became critical. Flash was sluggish one morning and did not want to get up. Laura left fresh water and a pile of grass clippings for him, but by the time she got home from school, he was feverish and his breathing was laboured.

"Oh, Flash," Laura moaned, her eyes welling with tears. "I'm so sorry. I don't know what to do. Does it hurt anywhere?"

Flash groaned. "It hurts everywhere. But please don't

fret, I'm sure I'll get better soon." He fell silent. Laura could hear him making the effort to pull breath into his lungs. His beautiful wings, usually folded neatly against his flanks, were splayed and crumpled.

"That's it," Laura sobbed. "I'm going to get some help." Flash raised his head and looked beseechingly at her with his golden eagle eyes, but was too weak to argue. His head sank back down. Maxine padded into the closet and sniffed her friend, then curled up in the cat bed beside him.

Laura called Krissy from the upstairs phone. "It's Flash," she said, desperation in her hushed voice. "He's really sick, Krissy. We have to do something. We're going to have to take him to an animal hospital or something. We can't keep him a secret any longer. I think he's dying."

"Why can't he just barf if he's got a stomach-ache?" Krissy asked.

"Horses can't throw up," Laura explained. "Their digestive tracts are a one-way street. They're not like cows."

Laura decided to call an emergency meeting of the Turtle Creek Triad. Both Krissy and Todd had to be involved in a major decision such as this. They arrived at Laura's house within minutes. The trio solemnly examined Flash as he lay on Laura's bed.

"You're right," Todd said. "I don't know anything about horses, but he doesn't look good at all."

"You know what this means, then," Laura said sadly, stroking Flash's emaciated form. "He won't be a secret from the world anymore and we'll probably lose him forever. But we can't just let him die." She choked back tears.

At this, Flash's head rose weakly, then dropped back. He coughed. It was a thick, sodden sound.

"Hang on a sec," Krissy said. She could always be counted on to be the voice of reason. "My brother is a veterinary student, you know. He's home from university for the holiday. We could ask him for help."

They discussed this possibility. "Can he be trusted?" Laura asked.

Krissy laughed humourlessly. "About this? I don't know, Laura. James is a really cool guy, but I've never asked him to examine a mythical creature before."

The decision was reached. Krissy walked quickly to the bedroom door. She paused, her hand on the doorknob. "I'll call you as soon as I've spoken to him," she promised.

Laura and Todd sat, comforted Flash and each other, and waited.

Chapter 12

Later that evening, Laura gently wrapped Flash in a soft towel, tucked him carefully into the backpack and transported the small patient to Krissy's house.

Krissy's brother James was waiting in the garage. He couldn't imagine what was so important that his sister had sworn him to absolute secrecy with tears in her eyes. He hoped the girls weren't in some sort of trouble. He glared suspiciously at Todd. He hadn't been thrilled to find a 14-year-old stranger living in his parent's house.

"Okay, kids, what's up?" James asked. The three looked at each other. Krissy nodded. Laura opened her backpack, laid the figure shrouded in the towel on the work bench and slowly peeled back the cloth.

James stared and leaned closer. The small animal

which lay in front of him was so still that at first he thought it was just one of those plastic models he knew Laura collected. Then he saw the rise and fall of the ribcage. It was breathing.

"Holy cow," James breathed. "*Holy cow...*"

"No, he's actually just a small horse," Laura said matter-of-factly. "But he's really sick and he needs help."

James stared at Flash for quite some time before snapping out of his shocked state. "Well, then," he said finally, standing. "I'd better get my bag."

The astounded brother was instantly replaced by the efficient veterinarian as James thoroughly examined the tiny patient. He fired off questions as he worked. "What has he been eating? How long has he been sick? When did the symptoms start getting worse? Who else knows about him?" He turned to Krissy. "Have you told Mom and Dad?" He looked at Laura. "Have you told *your* parents?" Both girls shook their head, ashamed.

James straightened up. "Okay, here's the deal. I think your little friend may have been poisoned. He's in really bad shape, I'm afraid. I'll treat him, but only if Laura promises to tell her parents about him—if he lives."

Todd and the girls exchanged horrified glances. "Poisoned?!"

"But how—" Laura began. She was interrupted by

James. "Do we have a deal?" he asked sternly.

Laura nodded miserably.

James flipped open his cell phone and punched in numbers. "Hi, Caroline?" he said. "James here. Yes, school is great, thanks. Listen, I know it's late, but I was wondering if I could use the lab at your clinic for a few minutes. I just have to run a couple of blood tests. It's for an assignment and I kind of got a bit behind in the last week. I still have the key."

Laura remembered that James had been the local veterinarian's assistant for a couple of summers before he went away to college. James and the vet chatted for a few more minutes, then he ended the call and said, "Let's rock."

James told his parents he was taking the kids to the vet clinic with him. "I need to run some tests for pathology class," he lied. "I thought they might learn find it interesting."

"See how easy it is to fudge the truth, Jimmy?" his sister hissed at him as they got into the car. "Now you know what we've been up against all summer."

~ ~ ~

Minutes later they were unlocking the back door of the vet clinic. A din of barking and meowing greeted their arrival. A parrot shrieked, making Laura jump. "Over here," James said, directing the three friends into a room with stainless steel examining tables, microscopes and a number of diagnostic machines.

"First thing we're going to do is draw some blood," James announced. Laura winced. She hated having blood taken, even though it never hurt as much as she thought it would. She stroked Flash's muzzle as James inserted a needle into his jugular vein. "It's okay, Flash," she whispered, her voice breaking. "It's okay."

As he worked, James listed Flash's symptoms.

"He has a rapid, weak pulse and his breathing is very shallow. And his mucous membranes are bluish. See?" He lifted Flash's upper lip to reveal his gums. Laura could see that they were indeed more blue than the usual healthy pink. "That means he's suffering from oxygen starvation. Bad sign. Has he had diarrhea?"

"Yes," Laura replied quietly. She felt sick. Oxygen starvation? That sounded very bad indeed.

"Now, we're going to give him an analgesic—a pain-killer—to make him more comfortable. Thing is, I'm not sure about the dosage..." James thought for a moment, then plunged the needle into a bottle of clear liquid and drew back a tiny amount of the fluid. "That should do it," he said with satisfaction as he depressed the plunger into the muscle of Flash's neck. Flash sighed.

How ironic, Laura thought helplessly as Flash lay unmoving on the table. *Flash has tried to save all of us lately, and now he's the one who needs rescuing.*

Laura had brought along a manure sample in a Ziplock bag, which James scrutinized under a microscope. He placed the vials of blood in a centrifuge, where they spun for some time. He then brushed smears onto slides for examination.

"Hmmmm," he said thoughtfully as he peered into the microscope. "His blood is very dark, almost chocolate-coloured. Interesting. Would I ever love to get this guy into the big lab at the university."

"That's exactly why I don't want to tell anyone!" Laura said angrily. "I'm afraid he'll be treated like a lab rat."

James ignored her outburst. Moments later he looked up and said, "Ladies and gentlemen, we have a winner. Just as I suspected, it's nitrate poisoning."

Laura stared at him blankly. "What is that?"

"Fertilizer. Your little friend has probably been eating grass that's been treated with fertilizer."

Laura suddenly remembered the empty sacks of weed-and-feed she'd seen in the garden shed. He had been eating the grass from the back lawn that she had cut for him. Why hadn't she made the connection?

"Is he going to be okay?" she asked, afraid of what the answer might be.

James shrugged his shoulders. "You've got to understand I've never treated anything like this. Even full-sized horses, as big as they are, are very fragile creatures. To be honest, the survival rate for this type of poisoning is very low. Very few animals recover. I'm sorry."

Laura gasped as the truth sank in. Hot tears sprang to her eyes, blurring her vision.

James explained. "Basically, nitrates turn to nitrites in the digestive system, and then ammonia, which becomes a protein. It gets into the bloodstream where it turns into a chemical that makes it hard for the blood to carry oxygen. The resulting tissue death is usually fatal for the animal."

The teens were stunned and silent.

"I'll give him a shot of methylene blue, which is the usual treatment for nitrate poisoning. He'll need plenty of fluids, because he's so dehydrated. He'll need lots of vitamin A, D and E, too. Beyond that, we'll just have to wait and see." He frowned at Laura. "I wish you had said something earlier."

Laura was wracked with guilt. She had been so intent on keeping Flash a secret, partly for her own selfish reasons. Now he was probably going to die—and it would be all her fault.

~ ~ ~

As they tidied the lab before leaving, James gathered up all the test samples to dispose of them. He hesitated a moment. The kids were busy fussing over Flash and were not paying the slightest attention to him. He quickly sealed one of the vials of blood, dated it, labeled it Sample F, added the words *Do Not Destroy* and placed it in the back of the small lab freezer. "Insurance," he said quietly to himself. "Just in case."

Chapter 13

That night, Laura smuggled Flash back into the house and made him as comfortable as possible in her closet. She shooed Maxi out of his bed, but the cat remained nearby as if she knew there was something wrong with her friend.

Early the next morning, Flash was no better. James had shown Laura how to intubate the tiny horse by running a small flexible hose down his throat and directly into his stomach. She had been pretty squeamish at first, but realized it was now up to her whether Flash lived or died. She carefully did as James had shown her, watching the side of his neck to make sure the tube was going into his esophagus and stomach and not into his windpipe and lungs. "You'll drown him if you make a mistake," James had warned her. Laura was even more terrified of that. She slowly dribbled a few drops of vitamin-rich water into a miniature funnel at the end of the hose. His breathing remained laboured, but normal. She sighed with relief and continued to pour the life-giving fluid into her tiny patient.

Laura told her mother she wasn't feeling well and wanted to stay home from school.

"What's the matter, hon?" her mother asked. Laura never asked to stay home; even if she had a bad cold she always wanted to go to school.

"I'm just feeling a bit punky. Really crampy, you know."

"Oh," her mother said, then, "Ohhh, I *see*. That kind of crampy." She winked.

Laura spent the entire day tending to Flash. By dinner time, he seemed no better. The tubing was causing his throat to become so sore that he couldn't even speak. Just a raw croaking noise escaped his muzzle the few times he attempted to talk. His pulse was still rapid and weak. A couple of times Laura could not even find his pulse, and her own heart skittered in her chest until she picked up its faint rhythm again. She was preparing herself for the worst, that he would not make it through another night.

~ ~ ~

Laura awoke, stiff and sore, on the floor of the closet the next morning. She had slept fitfully, waking often to make sure Flash was still breathing. His breath was so shallow that she had to place her ear next to his tiny nose to feel the short bursts of warm air against her earlobe.

She looked into the cat bed. Flash's eyes were open. He blinked. His breathing did not sound as tortured, although he still looked terribly emaciated. Laura felt the first pale glimmer of hope that her beloved friend was possibly going to live.

Laura was thankful it was a PD day, as she had no more excuses to offer for staying home. She called Krissy, who came over in the afternoon. By then, the dullness in Flash's eyes had been replaced by a brighter light, and he was even trying to drink on his own. Laura was especially relieved about that, as the whole tubing experience had been very stressful for her, let alone Flash.

That night, she bundled up her little patient again and took him back to Krissy's house. Down in the basement, James once again examined the little horse, checking his temperature, pulse and respiration.

"Better," he said. "Much better, actually."

Laura let out the breath she had been holding with a whoosh.

"He's going to be all right, then?" she asked, wanting so badly to believe it.

"Possibly. He's not out of the woods yet. Just keep giving him the vitamins, and keep him off the lawn until we've had some more rain. It's been a pretty dry autumn, so the fertilizer hasn't been washed into the ground yet. Also, plants—like grass—build up nitrates naturally on cloudy days and at night. I'm assuming he was only going out to graze in the dark, right?"

Laura nodded. She wondered if she could talk her parents into laying off the lawn chemicals altogether. Wasn't that stuff illegal these days anyway?

James reminded Laura of her promise. "You'll tell your parents now, right?"

Laura nodded. "Can I at least wait until Flash is completely better?"

James agreed.

Chapter 14

Laura doted over her little patient for the next couple of days. He thrived under her care, getting stronger every day. She made sure he drank lots of water, took his medicine and ate only the healthiest foods. His gaunt ribcage once again began to look well-fleshed and covered by a healthy, glossy coat.

By Thanksgiving Monday, Flash was flying blissfully around her bedroom to the strains of "Waltz of the Flowers," one of his favourite classical pieces from the Nutcracker Suite. Laura watched him hover and dive to the ebb and swell of the harp, strings and flutes, and knew it was time.

The house was fragrant with the smells of dinner cooking. Laura and her parents feasted on roast turkey, stuffing, cranberry sauce, squash, peas, mashed potatoes and gravy. There was both pumpkin pie and pecan pie with ice cream for dessert. The Connors loaded the dishwasher, tidied up the kitchen and collapsed onto couches and armchairs to digest dinner and watch some mindless reality show on TV.

"I've got the ultimate reality show right upstairs," Laura thought wryly about the mind-boggling surprise she was about to spring on her parents. She and Flash had discussed at great length how they were going to break the news. Flash was pleased that his mistress was going to tell her parents. Even though he was from a fantastic land many centuries in the past, he understood the importance of honesty, honouring your parents and keeping your word.

Laura reached for the remote and turned off the television. Tom and CeeCee looked at her questioningly. "What's up, honey?" her father asked.

Laura took a deep breath. "I need to talk to you both about something that happened months ago, and I should have spoken up way before this," Laura said, her voice strong and sure. "I've been lying about some stuff and I'm really sorry about that."

Her parents looked concerned. "Are you all right? Is it something serious?" her mother asked, getting to her feet.

"No, it's just—amazing and fabulous. And you'd better sit down," Laura said as a silver-winged form floated gracefully down the stairs, glided through the living room and landed gently on the footstool in front of her. Flash smoothed his elegant wings against his back and bowed deeply.

"Mom, Dad," Laura announced to her wide-eyed parents, "there's someone I want you to meet."

~ ~ ~

SUSAN STAFFORD-POOLEY
"The Fearless Editor"

Susan Stafford-Pooley was bitten by the horse bug at an early age, eventually owning a menagerie of hunters, jumpers, eventers, racehorses and ponies. She is the managing editor of *Horse Sport* magazine, Canada's largest English equestrian sport publication, and *Horsepower* magazine for horse-crazy kids. Susan has three grown children and lives on the shores of Lake Erie with her husband, Ross, a professional musician. *Pocket Pegasus: Flash and the Wings of Courage* is her second book.

Visit www.pocketpegasus.com.

Chapter 13

That night, Laura smuggled Flash back into the house and made him as comfortable as possible in her closet. She shooed Maxi out of his bed, but the cat remained nearby as if she knew there was something wrong with her friend.

Early the next morning, Flash was no better. James had shown Laura how to intubate the tiny horse by running a small flexible hose down his throat and directly into his stomach. She had been pretty squeamish at first, but realized it was now up to her whether Flash lived or died. She carefully did as James had shown her, watching the side of his neck to make sure the tube was going into his esophagus and stomach and not into his windpipe and lungs. "You'll drown him if you make a mistake," James had warned her. Laura was even more terrified of that. She slowly dribbled a few drops of vitamin-rich water into a miniature funnel at the end of the hose. His breathing remained laboured, but normal. She sighed with relief and continued to pour the life-giving fluid into her tiny patient.

Laura told her mother she wasn't feeling well and wanted to stay home from school.

"What's the matter, hon?" her mother asked. Laura never asked to stay home; even if she had a bad cold she always wanted to go to school.

"I'm just feeling a bit punky. Really crampy, you know."

"Oh," her mother said, then, "Ohhh, I *see*. That kind of crampy." She winked.

Laura spent the entire day tending to Flash. By dinner time, he seemed no better. The tubing was causing his throat to become so sore that he couldn't even speak. Just a raw croaking noise escaped his muzzle the few times he attempted to talk. His pulse was still rapid and weak. A couple of times Laura could not even find his pulse, and her own heart skittered in her chest until she picked up its faint rhythm again. She was preparing herself for the worst, that he would not make it through another night.